A CURSE OF THE HEART

ADELE CLEE

To Rose,
My wonderful mother and friend.
Our journey together is eternal.
With love always.

CHAPTER 1

*I*f Rebecca Linwood knew of a spell to turn a man into a mule, she would have used it on Gabriel Stone and then kicked his braying behind all the way around Hanover Square.

A gentleman was supposed to come to the aid of a damsel in distress, not slam the door in her face or threaten to drown her in the Thames.

Well, she would not give up so easily.

With a clenched fist, she hammered on the front door.

When the loud thud failed to rouse his butler, Rebecca decided she would have to find another way to get Mr. Stone's attention. So, with a curtsy and a friendly wave to the ogling groups of morning strollers, she plonked herself down on his front steps and contemplated her next move.

Perhaps she could scream at the top of her voice or dance an Irish jig; that would certainly attract attention. Perhaps she could accost the milkmaid and sneak in through the servants' quarters or mug a footman. His livery and powdered wig would provide an excellent disguise.

What would it take to get the gentleman to notice her?

What would it take to drag the grumpy old bear out of his cave?

Nothing, apparently.

From the corner of her eye, she noticed movement in the front window and turned to find her gaze locked with the gentleman in question.

He was much younger than she imagined. A scholar of the ancient world should surely have tufts of white hair sprouting out of every orifice, not the silky black locks of a Greek god. A scholar who spends most of his time huddled over his books should have pasty white skin, not the bronzed glow of an Italian Lothario. His eyes should be beady and black from hours spent reading in the dark, not wide and soulful, not the sort of warm brown that reminded her of horse chestnuts.

Of course, she expected him to be thin and scrawny. It was common knowledge scholars were often so engrossed in their studies they forgot to eat for days. However, this man's bulging shoulders filled the width of the window.

In fact, if Gabriel Stone wasn't so rude and ungentle-manly, she might have said he was handsome, in a classically rugged sort of way. In a way that may have appealed to her, had he possessed good manners.

Well, at least she had his attention.

The thought caused her chest to fill with pride as not everyone had her level of purpose and determination. That was until Mr. Stone gave her a disapproving glare and promptly closed the drapes.

With a disgruntled huff, she folded her arms across her chest. It was better to feel affronted than to let the tears fall.

But she could not bear another night like last night.

Her teeth chattered at the thought.

The noises started an hour after she had gone to bed, forcing her to sit up, her terrified gaze flitting around the

2

room, looking for the source of the mysterious sound. When she saw the shadow of a figure forming, she knew her mind was playing its tricks. The key to the door still hung on its black ribbon around her neck, the metal pressed flat against her skin as a comforting reminder.

The thought had not stopped her heart from racing.

This thing she feared was not bound by the usual laws of nature. A curse was not a physical being; it was not something that could be touched or reasoned with. It was nothing more than a whisper carried on a gentle breeze. It was a warning to those foolish enough to question its power and doubt its credibility.

Even with all her knowledge and experience, she had been foolish. She had read from the ancient Egyptian scroll as though reciting an ode while lounging in her bathtub.

Now, she was paying the price.

Gabriel Stone was the only person with the knowledge needed to break the evil curse. All she needed were a few mystical words of wisdom to revoke the incantation. It was not as though she wanted him to spill blood, or to dance under the moonlight wearing nothing more than a pair of deer antlers.

The sound of the front door opening interrupted her reverie. She shot to her feet, relief coursing through her veins. Perhaps the gentleman was not so cold-hearted after all.

But as Rebecca swung around she was met with the butler's solemn face. "I have been told to remind you that the maid will be washing the steps. That if you do not move, you will find yourself swimming in a river of suds all the way down to the Thames."

Did Mr. Stone think her a buffoon?

Did he think her someone who knocked on a stranger's door for the fun of it?

She was not deaf and had heard his warning the first time. Surely, the fact she was still standing there was proof that her cause was urgent, dire.

"I just need five minutes of his time, nothing more. Five minutes and then I'll be gone."

A look of pity flashed in the servant's eyes. But with a quick blink, it was gone. "You are wasting both time and energy. He will not see you, Miss Linwood. Good day."

"Please, wait. Please. I beg you."

Rebecca stared at the closed door. Hope abandoned her, leaving her faith in humanity shattered. She was going to have to find some other way to speak to Mr. Stone.

Dragging her feet as she ambled down the street, her thoughts drifted to the accident at her Egyptian museum, to Mr. Dempsey, the unfortunate gentleman who had dived out of the way of the flying bust of Nefertiti.

By way of an apology, she had confided in him and told him all about the ancient curse. He probably thought she was a candidate for Bedlam. But he had been polite and offered to introduce her to Mr. Stone, whom he assured her would be attending Lord Banbury's ball. All she needed to do was don her best gown. Mr. Dempsey would secure an invitation.

The idea left her in fits of laughter.

Thankfully, Mr. Dempsey was not offended when she explained she'd never been to a ball before and had no intention of ever doing so. She didn't even own a gown.

Now, it looked as though she had no other choice. She would have to rummage through her mother's things hoping to find something appropriate. She would have to wait for the bear to leave his cave and then she would pounce.

CHAPTER 2

*T*here was only one thing on Gabriel Stone's mind when he entered Lord Banbury's house. Only one thing could rouse his passion and cause the blood to pump rapidly through his veins—his studies.

"I think we all know why you're here." Banbury chuckled as Gabriel came to greet him. "We know what's dragged you out from the shadows."

Gabriel could not recall the last time he'd been out formally and felt like a stuffed partridge all trussed up in his evening attire. Even so, he forced a weak smile. "Well, it's not for the wine, whist or women."

It was for something far more exciting.

"Good," Banbury said, his gaze surveying the breadth of Gabriel's shoulders, as though the vast vision before him was a mirage. "Because the gentlemen outnumber the ladies tonight, and you are just too much of a distraction."

"Have no fear. The only thing I shall be surveying this evening is Bacanus' parchment," Gabriel replied in an attempt to show some interest in the conversation. He did not have time for idle chatter but refrained from being rude to his host. "Perhaps you should point me in the right direction, in case I get distracted along the way. As you say, that is the only reason I'm here."

Banbury laughed. "Oh, I don't want to spoil the thrill of the hunt, Stone," he said, patting Gabriel on the back. "It wouldn't do to have you miss out on all the fun. You'll have to search for the parchment yourself."

Gabriel suppressed a sigh. "If I'd known that, I would have brought the hounds."

If Banbury had lured him to the ball under a false pretext, he would drag him by his coattails all the way to London Bridge and dangle him headfirst from an arch.

Pushing his way through the crowded rooms, Gabriel recalled why he despised going about in Society. The feigned shrieks of laughter, the ostentatious dress and the exaggerated mannerisms were all merely masks of deception, an illusion to lure and entice the weak and feeble-minded.

Thankfully, he was not one of them.

He understood the game but chose not to play.

Deciding the study was the most obvious place to look and discovering the door unlocked, he peered inside. He knew Banbury kept the parchment stored in a display case. If it belonged to Gabriel, he would have it locked in a vault a hundred feet below ground. But after scanning the room for the third time, he could not locate the treasure.

Continuing down the hallway, he noticed another open door. The walls were lined from floor to ceiling with leather-bound books and so he thought to try there.

There were numerous groups of people milling about, none of them interested in the wooden lectern with the glass lid. Gabriel ignored them all, his eyes fixed on his target, his heart beating louder with every step. He'd waited years for this opportunity.

Like a fine wine, he drank in those first few lines slowly and let Becanus' words flow through him. He tried to banish every other thought from his mind. But the sound of laughter and raised voices cut through his concentration, so he could do nothing other than gaze upon its magnificence.

He was not sure how long he'd stood there, lost in a dream-like state, when he heard someone approach from behind and felt a light tap on the shoulder.

"I see you still have a morbid fascination with the dead."

Gabriel straightened and turned to see the familiar face of Lucas Dempsey. "And you're still creeping up on people." He removed his spectacles and brushed his hair from his brow. "As you're so light on your feet, perhaps you could use your talent to help me steal this. It is almost impossible to study it with all this noise and disruption, and I cannot persuade Banbury to part with it."

Lucas Dempsey shook his head. "This is a ball, Gabriel. There must be fifty ladies eager to get their hands on such a virile specimen. You should be dancing, not hunched over some ancient scroll."

"You know I'm not a man who wastes my time on such frivolities."

Gabriel examined Dempsey's countenance: his puffed-out chest, his chin held high and his determined gaze. This was not a chance meeting of old friends. Lucas Dempsey wanted something, and it was only a matter of time before he asked for it.

"What if I could persuade Banbury to give you more time to study the parchment? What if I could arrange for you to spend a whole day locked away in here?"

Gabriel's heart skipped a beat at the prospect, but he narrowed his gaze. "And why would you do that? What would you have me do in return?"

As expected, Lucas Dempsey came straight to the point. "I would have you speak to Miss Linwood. She has a problem at her museum and believes you are the only person who can help."

Were there no depths to how low Miss Linwood would stoop?

"I do not have time for fakes and frauds."

The fact she had thrown herself on his front steps conveyed a complete disregard for appropriate modes of conduct. It seemed anyone could open a museum and claim to have ancient relics. It took years of study to gain the knowledge needed to identify forgeries. No doubt someone duped the lady into purchasing crates of old junk.

"Everyone knows the lady is a charlatan," Gabriel continued.

Dempsey was too busy looking at his pocket watch to show any interest in his opinion of Miss Linwood.

"That is a shame," he said. "Well, as much as I enjoy discussing your interest in antiquities, I have an urgent desire to stroll around the garden. I'm afraid it cannot wait."

Mr. Dempsey excused himself and walked towards the door. Gabriel's palms began to itch, and his fingers throbbed. Dempsey only wanted him to talk to the lady. A brief conversation was the only thing required to gain more time to study Becanus' theory on hieroglyphics. It would also give him an opportunity to confirm his suspicions, a chance to prove that Miss Linwood knew as much about ancient Egypt as he knew about petticoats and pins.

"Very well. I shall speak to your Miss Linwood, but nothing more. In return, I want two whole days with no disruptions."

"Done." Lucas Dempsey gave a little chuckle. "Well,

there's no time like the present. I believe you'll find the lady in the ballroom."

Left alone with his treasure, Gabriel did not want to leave the parchment. The voice in his head told him it would take but one more glance to commit it to memory. Like an addict in need of opium, he scoured the images: the eye, the vulture, the snake, and then another thought struck him, forcing him to straighten.

What if Lucas Dempsey changed his mind?

Perhaps he should find Miss Linwood, hear what she had to say and be done with it. As a gentleman, Dempsey would have no choice but to fulfil his part of the bargain.

The lure of having two days to study in peace dragged him from the room towards the sound of music and laughter. It was not difficult to find her. He had watched her sitting on his front steps and had no problem picking her out.

Miss Linwood shone like a bright beacon in the crowded ballroom. Her figure was tall and lithe, her narrow waist curving up into a generous bosom. Her emerald-green gown highlighted the stark contrast of her fiery copper curls. There was something regal about her countenance, something proud and noble.

Gabriel groaned inwardly.

He would need to be firm with her. He would listen to her plea, feign interest and then make his apology.

Of course, she would have no choice but to accept it, once he had shamed her with his little test.

She turned to her companion and laughed, her mouth curling into a tempting smile, her eyes shining with amusement. The brilliance of it all hit him so hard in the chest he was forced to take a breath.

Damn.

He did not need this sort of distraction.

Thank God the lady was a charlatan and a fraud.

Rebecca noticed him standing in the doorway, his broad shoulders filling the space. She had seen the same disapproving stare this morning, the same irritated glare. Only now, it appeared he was trying to attract her attention. The gentleman confirmed her suspicion when he raised his hand and beckoned her to follow him.

"What is the matter, Miss Linwood?" Miss Ecclestone asked. Her companion was betrothed to Lucas Dempsey and had also escaped being hit by the flying bust of Nefertiti.

"The gentleman standing in the doorway is Mr. Stone."

Miss Ecclestone turned and followed her gaze. "Good heavens. He is waving his hand at you like a master summoning a disobedient dog. I suggest you stay here and wait for him to find his manners."

If an hour sitting on a cold step was anything to go by, Mr. Stone had no manners.

Rebecca met his hard, assessing gaze. Her instincts told her that if she missed this opportunity, he would not make the offer again.

"It is imperative I speak to him," she said, the sense of urgency in her voice unmistakable, as she imagined being woken again by the torturous groans and rattling bed. "I would not expect you to understand, Miss Ecclestone, but I have no choice. I must go to him."

Ignoring her companion's wide eyes, Rebecca pushed her way through the crowd, pulled along by an invisible rope, her mind oblivious to any noise or distraction. Her steps only faltered when she was within a foot of Mr. Stone.

If there was a man in the world whose name perfectly

portrayed his character, it was Gabriel Stone. He was tall and broad, his body as strong and as hard as granite, his muscular arms carved to perfection, his jaw rigid and unrelenting. Her gaze swept over him from head to toe. But he did not yield under such scrutiny.

With a whip-like flick of the wrist, he brushed his black hair from his brow in an act of defiance. As she stared into those sinful brown eyes, she bit down on her bottom lip. Then she saw the veil fall, saw his gaze soften, if only for a moment.

Excellent, she thought, watching him blink rapidly to replace it.

"Mr. Stone," she began, her tone conveying an inner confidence. "I am Miss Linwood. I called on you this morning. You shooed me away from your steps with the threat of being washed to the Thames in a stream of soapy suds."

Gabriel Stone did not reply. He did not even have the decency to look embarrassed. But as his gaze drifted over her face, she felt a sudden jolt of awareness that forced her to swallow.

"Come with me, Miss Linwood," he said, taking her by the elbow and guiding her along the busy corridor.

Rebecca ignored the raised brows and gaping glances. To keep up with his long strides, she had no choice but to totter along behind him. In his impatience, she imagined him throwing her over his shoulder or waving a crude club as he grabbed her hair and dragged her off to his cave.

"Where are we going?" she asked, wondering if she had pinned all her hopes on a man who was clearly insane.

"To talk."

His reply was cold and blunt and suddenly the noises at night didn't seem quite so terrifying.

Mr. Stone strode into the library. Seeing it was empty, he

let go of her elbow and closed the door. He retrieved a pair of spectacles from the inside pocket of his coat, fiddled with the wire and put them on.

"Do you mind telling me what this is?" he said, pointing to a lectern.

Rebecca couldn't concentrate on the piece of wooden furniture. Her heart pounded in her chest. In his spectacles, Gabriel Stone looked wise and scholarly while his firm jaw and full lips presented a perfectly wicked contradiction.

Dismissing the odd feeling the vision roused, she walked towards him. "I think you'll find it's a display case in the shape of a lectern. I imagine it is used for—"

"Not the lectern," he said with mild irritation. "Can you tell me what's inside?"

Rebecca stepped closer and peered into the glass case. "Why? Don't you know?"

"Of course I know," he said with a dismissive wave. "I want to know if you do."

Did he think her a fool? How could someone with an interest in Egyptian antiquities not know of Becanus?

"Oh, that. It is a sixteenth-century parchment detailing the transcription of the pictorial language of the ancient Egyptians."

Gabriel Stone raised an arrogant brow. "Lord Banbury could have told you that."

"Becanus dedicated his life to deciphering their language," she added.

"A textbook answer, Miss Linwood."

Ignoring his tempting countenance, she thrust her hands on her hips. "What exactly is the problem here, Mr. Stone? What is it that disturbs you? That I am a woman or that I possess a modicum of intelligence?" When his mouth fell open, she added, "Of course, you must know Becanus' theory is flawed."

The muscles in his jaw twitched and his lips thinned. "I am aware of Becanus' interpretation, Miss Linwood. But I am interested to hear your opinion."

He was not interested in her opinion at all.

This was a test to undermine her position. Gabriel Stone wanted to make her look foolish. He wanted to trample all over her until she knew her place.

Her chest grew warm, and it became hard to swallow. But it had nothing to do with the proximity of his powerful body. Small bubbles were forming in her blood, simmering and popping until she wanted to put her hands around his throat and throttle the man.

"Becanus' theory is based on a symbolic translation," she said, slapping him across the face with her gloved opinion. "Whereas, with the discovery of the Rosetta Stone, we now know the pictographic script is more representative of sound."

He narrowed his gaze, his brown eyes intense and focused as though thirsty to hear more. "Anything else?"

"What do you want me to say, Mr. Stone? That one must consider many facets when studying hieroglyphics: alphabet signs, syllabic signs … must I go on? Must I tell you that I can translate the Coptic language? Must I stand here and provide a detailed list of my credentials in order to appease your warped sense of curiosity?"

Gabriel Stone sucked in a breath. "You can translate Coptic?"

"Of course," she replied with an arrogant wave.

He closed the gap between them and the air crackled with some undefinable force. Under the scrutiny of his gaze, she felt like an exhibit in her own museum.

"Who are you?" he whispered. His face was so close to hers she could feel his soft breath caress her skin. She could not take her eyes off his lips as some fanciful notion of being kissed filled her head. The thought melted her ice-cold shield to warm her lonely heart.

When he shook his head and stepped back, she suddenly felt more alone than ever, the few feet feeling as wide as a ravine.

"I am just a stupid woman," she said, anger and bitterness woven through every word. She had made another mistake in seeking this gentleman out.

"Anyone who can translate Coptic is far from stupid."

"I am not an expert in the ways of the Egyptians, Mr. Stone. I do not profess to be a scholar. Indeed, I only wish I were, as I have made a terrible, terrible mistake."

Gabriel Stone removed his spectacles, his gaze sharp. "Why? What have you done?"

"I have read from an ancient scroll, and now I fear I am cursed."

CHAPTER 3

"*I* am cursed, Mr. Stone, and I implore you to find a way to break the spell."

Gabriel stared at her, his mouth hanging open while his mind conjured strange images involving deadly serpents, thunderbolts of fire and plagues of locusts.

He shook his head.

A curse!

The woman had been reading too many Gothic novels and frightened herself half to death.

"Contrary to what you may have read, Miss Linwood, there is no such thing as a curse. Not an Egyptian one, at any rate."

She took another step, closing the gap between them as suppressed emotion burst forth. "Do these eyes lie?" she cried. "Do you not see the red lines? Do you not see how they are sore and swollen from lack of sleep?"

Gabriel witnessed nothing other than the most captivating, most vibrant green eyes he had ever seen. They reminded him of ripe apples and lush summer meadows, of gaiety and laughter. Indeed, he found it hard to focus on anything else and had to drag his thoughts back to the present, had to force himself to examine her countenance.

She seemed different now, conveying a level of vulnerability so opposed to the confident, defiant lady who'd sat on his front steps. It was hard to believe she was the same lady who had shone with brilliance in the ballroom. And he found the contrast intriguing.

"Look at them, Mr. Stone." She thrust herself forward as she pointed to the offending lines. "Are they not evidence enough?"

"Yes," he whispered, not really seeing anything at all. Perhaps it was all a figment of her wild imagination. "I do not deny the Egyptians believed in curses. On the contrary, as I am sure you know, they used them on tombs to protect the dead and as a way of preventing looters." He softened his tone. "But there is no record of such things ever affecting the living, no record of anyone ever suffering from a curse."

She sucked in a deep breath. "I know what I have seen, Mr. Stone."

His traitorous gaze could not help but glance down at the mounds of soft, creamy flesh swelling and rising up to meet him in all their wondrous glory.

Bloody hell!

For a moment, he felt deprived of air and had to shake his head to regain focus. These were precisely the sort of temptations he avoided. Such distractions appeased the body but plagued the mind.

This lady was dangerous, and he needed to get rid of her. Now.

It should not be too difficult to convince her of her error, to prove her fears were a result of her own creation. Once he had examined all the facts, there would be a rational explanation.

"This ancient scroll you mentioned. The one you read. How did you come by it?"

"I found it in a wooden crate," she said, her eyes reflecting a level of gratitude that he had bothered to ask the question, "along with the staff. Most of my father's objects are on display at the museum. But there are still some items in the storeroom that need sorting and recording. I found the crate in there."

Her father's objects?

Gabriel knew the location of all the genuine Egyptian relics. He scoured the recesses of his mind to recall someone with the same surname who had an interest in Egyptology. "And your father is—"

"Dead, Mr. Stone. My mother, too."

He felt an instant tug in his chest. The feeling one gets when meeting someone whose fate had followed a similar path to one's own.

"As are mine," he replied, for no other reason than to acknowledge the similarity.

Her eyes searched his face as though looking for a sign that the thought still pained him. "I do not recall seeing the scroll on the list of inventory," she said, returning to the matter. "Indeed, I have never seen it before. Perhaps that's why I doubted its authenticity. Why I foolishly read from it without fear of reprisal."

"We are all guilty of foolishness," he found himself saying, wondering why he felt the need to offer comfort. He was still trying to fathom out why a woman with her intelligence would believe in such a ridiculous notion.

Miss Linwood managed a weak smile. "But I should have known better. I should not have doubted the power of the dead to exact their revenge on the living."

The rattling of the door handle drew his attention, the

sudden noise causing Miss Linwood to jump, her hand flying to her chest as the other grasped his arm.

"There is nothing to fear, Miss Linwood," he said, trying to determine which thought disturbed him the most. Was it the thought that such an erratic action was a sure sign she truly was suffering from a curse? Or the fact he felt desire shoot through his body at the speed of a lightning bolt.

When the door burst open, even he was relieved to see the curious gazes of a young lady and her male companion. What was he expecting? The towering figure of Anubis dangling a pair of weighing scales?

Witnessing the room was occupied, and with a fit of the giggles, the lady dragged her admirer back out into the corridor.

Miss Linwood breathed a sigh of relief and promptly let go of his sleeve. "Forgive me, Mr. Stone. I'm afraid my wits appear to have abandoned me."

His wits had all but up and left him, too. It was imperative he focused on the task. "If you read from the scroll, can I assume it was written in English or Coptic?"

"English." She nodded. "It was written in English."

"Was it written on papyrus, parchment, vellum?"

Tiny furrows appeared on her brow and after a brief silence, she said, "No, Mr. Stone. It was not written on papyrus or vellum."

Gabriel shrugged his shoulders and threw his hands up in the air. "Well, there you have it then. The scroll does not appear to be Egyptian at all. And if it is not Egyptian, then there can be no curse."

There. Now he had solved the problem he could put this tempting lady far from his mind and continue with his research.

Miss Linwood simply stared at him, her face ghastly pale

as though drained of all blood. She blinked a few times, and he noticed her eyes brimming with tears. "Then I am sorry to have troubled you, Mr. Stone. I am sorry to have wasted your time."

She turned abruptly, picking up her green silk skirt as she hurried towards the door. Before he knew what was happening, he caught her by the arm and pulled her back around to face him.

"Surely, you understand the logic in my questioning," he said, feeling a strange urge to banish those tears, to see her eyes bright and bold once again. "Surely, you understand how the mind can play its tricks. How easy it is in times of fear to believe in the illogical."

"I do," she replied, "but you have not heard the cries. You have not felt your bed shake, felt the floor shudder beneath your feet." She sucked in a breath, and he could see she was shaking. "Two people almost died, Mr. Stone, and it is my fault." Anger surfaced as she yanked her arm free from his grasp, anger mixed with a look of disappointment and she struggled to meet his gaze. "It is not your concern. I was mistaken. You are not the man I hoped you would be."

Gabriel let her go.

She ran out into the hallway, yet he did nothing.

Her words hurt like a fresh sting. His body throbbed and ached with his own inadequacy. It was not a new feeling. He had lived with the same pain for years. Had he been any other man, he would have chased after her, pulled her into an embrace, eased her fears and pledged his help.

Yet even in his melancholic mood, he could not quash the urge to return to his work. He could not abandon the need to fulfil his ambition. And so he wandered over to the parchment and let Becanus be his solace. Studying the ancient world was the only thing he knew how to do.

When the old words failed to rouse his interest, he glanced back over his shoulder and stared at the open door.

Perhaps he should visit Miss Linwood's museum and try one last time to convince her of her error. Perhaps he would find something of interest amongst the relics, something to nurture his passion, something to feed his obsession. Then he would walk away from her, happy in the knowledge he had done his best.

CHAPTER 4

*G*abriel stood outside Miss Linwood's museum, an elegant townhouse in Coventry Street, and surveyed the exterior.

His first thought was that her father must have been wealthy, or perhaps she had a gentleman sponsor whose interest extended beyond the preservation of historical objects. Feeling the urge to banish the thought from his mind, he focused on the facade. The impressive Doric columns supporting the portico reflected the character of its owner perfectly, as they suggested pride, strength and a wealth of wisdom.

Miss Linwood had impressed him with her knowledge of Becanus. If she truly could translate Coptic script, then she may prove to be a valuable asset. This, he decided, was the reason he sought her out. He would help her to see that the curse was something concocted by the imagination. In return, she would make herself available should he find himself in need of a translator.

After paying the entrance fee, he wandered around the downstairs rooms, moving past an array of nautical paintings as he had no interest in them. Then he discovered that the Egyptian antiquities were on the upper floor. So he decided to peruse the objects, in the hope of clarifying whether the lady was a fraud or a person to be admired in their field of expertise.

There were more than twenty people milling about upstairs, browsing the various display cases and plinths supporting masks and statues. In an area separated by a length of red rope, there was an assortment of stone tablets, some of them as tall and as wide as a man.

Without revealing his impatience, he waited to examine the first display, disappointed to find nothing but an old tooth-pick and ivory combs carved into the shapes of animals. The display of canopic jars proved to be a little more interesting, and he scanned the cards to check for errors.

"Do you have a particular interest in canopic jars, Mr. Stone?"

Her soft, melodic tone caused the hairs on his nape to tingle. When he turned to face her, he was surprised to find her wearing a rather dreary-looking dress.

"I have an interest in anything Egyptian, Miss Linwood." He tried to remain emotionless while scanning the brown ensemble that did nothing to enhance the shape of her figure.

Her gaze followed his, falling to the plain material. "Visitors pay to see the exhibition, Mr. Stone," she said as though she could hear his thoughts. "And so I do my utmost to move about here unnoticed."

The image of her generous bosom encased in green silk flashed into his mind, and he blinked to dismiss it. He glanced into those luscious emerald eyes, moving up to the mass of rich copper curls. A man would have to be blind not to notice her. Even in such dull attire, she had an inherent sensuality that called out to him. It was there in the way she spoke, in the way she walked, in the way her face revealed the emotion behind every word. Then his mind added further weight to his assessment, for he imagined her sweet body welcoming him, imagined the feel of that first delicious thrust.

"Bloody hell," he muttered in frustration, pushing his hand through his hair by way of a distraction.

"Is there something wrong, Mr. Stone?"

Yes, damn it, everything was wrong. He should have stayed at home, his rampant mind engaged in his books.

"I said you've done well, Miss Linwood," he replied, making a quick recovery. "I particularly like the jars in the shape of the four sons of Horus."

She smiled. "I'm rather fond of the jackal, although I cannot claim the credit for their discovery. Surely, as a scholar of Egyptology, this is not your first visit to the exhibition?"

What was he supposed to say? That he had sworn never to set foot in the place and expected her to be a dimwit with a crate full of forgeries? He wondered if her question was intended to force him to reveal the reason behind his visit.

"Yes, this is my first visit." He decided to reserve his opinion until he had assessed the evidence.

"Then let me direct you to the stone tablets, they are most impressive." She hesitated, perhaps waiting for him to offer his arm, but then led the way while he followed. "As you probably know, this one depicts the weighing of one's heart against the feather of Ma'at." She gave him a moment to study it before pointing to the next one. "And here we have servants praying to Osiris and Imentet."

The sight of the second tablet sent a cold chill sweeping over him. He had seen these tablets before. He had studied them and had lengthy discussions with their owner, who most certainly was not Miss Linwood.

Feeling a surge of anger infused with the sour taste of disappointment, he jumped over the rope, ran his palm over the ancient stone and pressed the tips of his fingers into the powdery indentations.

"Mr. Stone," Miss Linwood gasped. She glanced over her shoulder and stamped her foot. "Visitors are not allowed to touch the objects, surely you know that."

Gabriel sneered, revealing his resentment that she had thought him a fool. "But these are not your objects, are they, Miss Linwood?" He sounded like a snake spitting its venom, warning its prey to consider its next move carefully as his bite was known to be deadly.

She looked shocked, and a little confused. "What on earth are you talking about?" she whispered through gritted teeth. "Come out of there at once, before someone sees you."

"I would like to speak to you in private." Arrogance dripped from every word, his tone conveying his disdain for liars and cheats. "Now, if you please, Miss Linwood."

Miss Linwood put her hands on her hips. "Mr. Stone. I have neither the time nor the inclination to listen to the ramblings of a madman. Now get out of there."

Gabriel stepped back over the rope and came to stand in front of her. "Oh, you will listen or else I shall tell everyone here that these tablets do not belong to you. I shall tell everyone that I believe them to be stolen."

She took a step closer, so the tops of their toes were touching, and offered a confident smile. "Then you had better follow me."

Rebecca should have thrown the gentleman out, but she knew how one's passion often manifested in the strangest of ways.

"This way, Mr. Stone." She marched along the corridor towards her office, aware of the power emanating from the man chasing her heels. She could feel his angry gaze lashing at her back and shoulders, each whip desperate to draw blood, each short, ragged breath mimicking her own erratic heartbeat.

"Sit down, Mr. Stone," she said, waving her hand at a chair while she took the seat behind the desk, grateful there was a large, solid object between them.

"How did you come to own those tablets?" he demanded.

Rebecca wondered if he was always so blunt and direct. She was of a mind to tell him to go to the devil. But the need to see him grovel, to see those eyes soften when delivering his apology, was far too much of a temptation.

"I have already told you. My father left them to me in his will. He also paid for this house and every item you see in it." Presenting him with her most dazzling smile, she added, "Would you care to see the papers before you pass sentence or will you throw me in the gallows with no hope of reprieve?"

Gabriel Stone narrowed his gaze and shuffled to the edge of the chair. "Those tablets belong to the estate of Lord Wellford. They do not belong to you. If they had been sold, I would have known about it."

Rebecca pursed her lips. He looked devilishly handsome when he was annoyed, and her stomach did little flips as she knew what was coming next. "Yes. You are quite right, Mr. Stone. The tablets belonged to the Wellford estate, but now they belong to me."

He threw his hands up in the air. "That is not possible. I know the family personally. I do not think—"

"Frankly, Mr. Stone, I do not care what you think. Everything you see belongs to me. I have proof. So let that be an end to the matter."

With a deep sigh, Mr. Stone threw himself back in the chair. Despite his rude manner, a part of her felt sad that they could not converse more civilly. They had lost their parents, they shared an interest in the ancient world, and as much as she tried to suppress it, she felt oddly drawn to him.

"Lord Wellford was my mentor, Miss Linwood," he said, as though it was the only explanation needed. "He would never have permitted the sale of his most treasured possessions."

"Lord Wellford was my father, Mr. Stone. And I agree. He would never have permitted anyone to sell them."

He straightened. "Your father? I recall there being three sons and a wife but—"

Unable to stop the surge of emotion, Rebecca jumped from the chair. "Please do not tell me I am wrong about that. I think I know my own father. You have come to my museum and accused me of being a thief and a fraud. You have intimated I am a feather-brained fool who has convinced herself she is cursed. Had my father been your friend and mentor, as you claim, then he would have been thoroughly ashamed of you, sir."

She sat back down, her legs giving way under the strain.

Mr. Stone gripped the arms of his chair and swallowed audibly as he stared off into the distance. After a brief moment, he blinked. "Forgive me, Miss Linwood. You are right. Lord Wellford would have called me out for such disgraceful conduct." He took a deep breath and looked at her directly. "You must understand. The study of the ancient world … well, it is all I know."

His voice brimmed with emotion, the tone revealing a

level of tenderness she had not seen in him before. Once again, she felt a tug in her chest. She wondered what it would feel like to have those muscular arms wrapped around her, to have those strong hands caress her body, to feel safe, warm and protected.

"I understand," she said, the need to placate him now stronger than the need for self-preservation. "It is all I know, too."

They sat there in silence, neither knowing what to say next. The overriding thought in her head was that she did not want him to go. It made no sense. Mere minutes ago she would have pushed him down the stairs with her boot attached to his behind.

"Perhaps we should start again, Mr. Stone," she said, feeling rather magnanimous. "It would be nice to have someone to call upon should I have a problem with one of the relics. To be able to speak to someone who understands my father's work would be invaluable."

His lips thinned. "I was not very helpful when you asked for advice last night, Miss Linwood."

"Linwood is my grandmother's name," she clarified, noting the inflection in his tone when he spoke her name. "I prefer to use it for reasons I do not care to go into. And no, you were not very helpful at all. I am grateful, however, that we had a chance to speak." When a frown marred his brow, she added, "In arriving home late last night I appeared to have missed the haunting. It was the first proper night's sleep I've had in over a week."

His gaze drifted over her hair and face, lingered on her lips and when it skimmed the outline of her breasts, she suddenly felt a little warmer inside.

"If you still need my help with the curse," he began, his

tone soft and rich, just the way she liked it, "then I will gladly assist in any way I can."

Relief shot through her. She clasped her hands to her chest, feeling a renewed sense of optimism in his abilities. "Thank you, Mr. Stone. You do not know how happy I am to hear you say that."

His mouth curved into the beginnings of a smile. It was the most wonderful thing she had ever seen.

"Would you like to see the scroll or perhaps the staff in the crate?" she said.

He steepled his fingers and held them to his lips, his brows drawn together in concentration. "I would like to consider all the facts without prejudice. When you say hauntings, what do you mean?"

"It is as I mentioned last night. I hear noises coming from the storeroom—"

"You live here?" He did not hide his surprise.

Rebecca nodded. "Yes. My rooms are on the third floor."

"I see. Forgive me. Please continue."

When she smiled at him, he sucked in a breath. "It is the same every night," she explained. "I hear whispers, scratching and moaning and then the bed shakes."

He looked at her a little dubiously. "And this all began when you read from the scroll?"

She nodded.

"This is highly inappropriate, I know, but if I may be so bold as to ask, are you alone when you experience the bed shaking?"

Rebecca's eyes widened. "Of course I am alone! What are you suggesting? That I am plagued by a phantom lover?"

Mr. Stone coughed into his fist, and she could not decide if he had something stuck in his throat or if he was laughing. "Please disregard the question. And I am correct in saying that every night you experience the same thing," he reaffirmed. When she nodded again, he asked, "Do you think I would be able to hear these strange noises?"

"Oh, yes. I am certain you would. If you were to hear them, too, then I would know I am not losing my mind. If you are free, you may call this evening and then you will be sure to hear them. My housekeeper leaves at nine, and I am on my own all night until eight."

Rebecca noticed him swallow deeply. Now she thought of it, she sounded more than a little desperate.

"When you say you are on your own, I assume you have a maid. Has she heard a similar thing, too?"

"No, Mr. Stone. When I say I am on my own, I mean I am alone."

He muttered a curse and looked at everything in the room except her, and then he scratched his head and sighed. "Very well, I shall come this evening. The sooner the matter is finished with the better. What I mean is only then will you be able to sleep again at night."

"Wonderful. Mrs. James leaves through the front door. She is always the last one here and has never stayed past nine thirty. I trust by your response there is no one to object to you spending the evening here?"

He stood abruptly as though the question caused him discomfort. "I live alone, Miss Linwood, and I work alone. So no, there is no one to offer any objection." He gave her a respectful bow. "Until tonight."

"Until tonight," she repeated, feeling a flutter in her stomach at the prospect of having company this evening.

He walked to the door but then turned back to face her. "If you could provide a list of all those who work here, at what times they have access and anything else you might think pertinent."

Rebecca had no idea why he was interested in that information but thought it best to say nothing. "I shall provide you with everything you need."

He managed a smile. "And I trust there is no one to object to my presence here this evening."

She looked up at his handsome face, into eyes that made her forget to breathe. "Like you, there is no one to object. Like you, I am alone."

CHAPTER 5

*G*abriel was not a gentleman to hover on a street corner at night or hide behind a bush spying on the home of an unmarried lady. That sort of licentious conduct was reserved for bucks and rakes, not respectable scholars of the ancient world. Yet here he was dressed in black, waiting to partake in a late night rendezvous.

But this was not a rendezvous, he reminded himself.

This was penance, to atone for the disgraceful way he'd behaved.

Lord Wellford had been a man of patience, a man sympathetic to the needs of his students. He'd bought Gabriel books, paid for dinner, listened to his theories on the mummification process. And now he would repay the kindness of his mentor by coming to the aid of his daughter.

Thirty minutes had passed since the housekeeper let herself out through the front door and waddled off down the street with her wicker basket swinging on her arm. Gabriel had hung back in the shadows, to wait and ensure no one else entered the house without Miss Linwood's knowledge. It was also wise to wait until he could enter the building unnoticed.

He still found the thought of her living alone rather unsettling. Why employ a housekeeper who leaves at nine? Why not hire a maid or paid companion? Once he'd dealt with the curse, which probably amounted to nothing more than an infestation of rats, he would convince Miss Linwood of the need for a chaperone at night.

Walking up to the door, he took a deep breath and rapped three times.

She opened it immediately. Her radiant expression suggested someone eagerly awaiting the arrival of a friend, not a man set on disproving her theory, ready to leave her looking like a naive fool.

"Mr. Stone." She stepped back to bid him entry. "Please, come in." As her gaze drifted over his attire, she smiled. "Black suits you."

He ran his hand down the front of his coat, intrigued by the compliment. Handing her his hat and gloves he decided to offer one of his own.

"And I find white much prettier than brown."

She blushed as she glanced down at the pale muslin dress. The silver-green bodice complemented the vibrancy of her copper curls.

"Well, it is more appropriate for an unmarried lady, as opposed to the dress I wore to Lord Banbury's ball. That one was my mother's as I do not own a ball gown of my own."

The memory of how exquisite she looked in emerald green, how the material clung to her soft curves, made his mouth feel so parched he feared his top lip had stuck to his gum.

"White is very fetching, Miss Linwood," he heard himself say and then wanted to kick himself in the shin for sounding so pathetic.

"Have you eaten, Mr. Stone?"

The answer was yes. But for some unfathomable reason, he said, "No, Miss Linwood. I have not."

"Excellent." She beamed. "I took the trouble of having Mrs. James prepare a light supper. Under the guise that I was so ravenous this evening, I would need a much larger portion. I'm sure there will be something amongst the assortment that will appeal to your appetite."

While his face presented an affable smile, the voice in his head screamed for him to run, screamed for him to banish all the lustful thoughts clawing away at his needy body. He should be at home, reading or studying, or doing anything other than spending more time in the company of a flame-haired temptress.

"You should not have gone to any trouble," he muttered, his gaze locked on the tempting sight of shapely ankles as he followed her up to the top floor.

"I'm afraid I have no formal dining room, so we shall have to eat in here."

As she led him into the room, he sucked in a breath.

It was as though he had spent years roaming the darkness only to stumble upon a dazzling celestial palace. The room sparkled with light and vitality, and his eyes drank in the sight. The marble and gilt furniture, the white walls, and the abundance of mirrors all made the room feel alive. It was as if it had a life beyond what the eye could see.

Miss Linwood noticed his open mouth. "My mother was an actress. Most of what you see belonged to her." She waved her hand around the room. "She had a certain way about her, an illuminating presence that is reflected in this room. I have her hair, but that is where the likeness ends."

She was wrong.

She had an illuminating presence, too. He could see it and feel it. Her undeniable sensual appeal was more potent than any opiate. He glanced at the painting above the mantel, at the face of an angel in the guise of Cleopatra.

"Is that your mother?"

Miss Linwood smiled, her face revealing genuine affection. "Yes. She was renowned for her performance of Cleopatra, which as you can imagine pleased my father no end."

He stared at the painting, his thoughts drawn to Lord Wellford, to the man who had lived a double life. The man he obviously did not know very well at all.

Perhaps sensing an element of disquiet, she said, "My mother and father were in love, Mr. Stone. While I cannot approve of the circumstance they found themselves in, I cannot condemn them for following their hearts."

"No." The word was but a whisper. Now was not the time to drag up painful memories of his childhood.

"Come, let us eat," she said, and he was grateful for the distraction.

They sat at a small mahogany table, talked of their love for the ancient world, nibbled on cold beef and drank too much claret. There were no awkward silences, no reprisals for breaches of etiquette and he almost forgot he'd only come to chase away the rats.

"Would you care for another drink, Mr. Stone?"

"No, thank you, Miss Linwood." He put his hand over the glass to curb the temptation. Besides, he needed a clear head if he was to convince her nothing sinister was going on here.

She glanced up at the clock on the mantel. "Well, it is after eleven. Perhaps we should take our places. I think it best I follow my usual routine."

"And what is your usual routine?"

"Well, I wash and change out of my clothes. I lock the door to my chamber and wear the key on a ribbon around my neck."

She put her hand to her throat, her delicate fingers tracing the line of the imagined ribbon and suddenly the tips of her fingers became the tip of his tongue. "Then I climb into bed and wait."

Lord above. He needed another glass of claret. A large one. Preferably a bottle.

To focus his attention, he jumped out of his chair and picked up the candlestick from the middle of the table.

"Very well. Let's go to your chamber and take our places."

With a spring in her step, Miss Linwood led him towards the door. But then she stopped abruptly, forcing him to cover the flame with his hand for fear of being plunged into darkness.

"But you cannot come inside my chamber." Her face flushed a pretty shade of pink. "I do not think it would be appropriate."

Gabriel suppressed a grin. If he wanted to ravish her, he did not need to be in her bedchamber to do so. To prove his theory, his mind concocted the perfect image of a naked Miss Linwood stretched out on the chaise.

"You do not need to un-undress," he said, stumbling over the word. "But I do need to be with you when you hear the noises." By way of reinforcing his point, he added, "It is the only way to be certain we hear the same things."

She frowned as she scanned him from head to toe.

"May I remind you that you invited me here," he continued. "You asked me to help you solve the mystery of the ancient curse." He sounded somewhat dramatic. But he refused to admit it had taken no effort to persuade him to come this evening.

"You're right." She lifted her chin. "Come, Mr. Stone. You may follow me."

Miss Linwood took the candlestick from his hand and with a swish of her skirt went out into the hallway.

The shabby corridor felt dark and oppressive as opposed to the feeling of pure decadence created in the drawing room. Gabriel wondered what the decor in her bedchamber would reveal about her character.

As she opened the door, he noticed her hand tremble. Did the room remind her of her nightmares or was it his presence in such an intimate space that affected her most?

Gabriel followed her inside, watched her light the candelabra at her bedside and despite all his pious protestations, thoughts of seduction swamped his mind.

The decor in the room did not help matters. The red walls, the deep-red hangings on the canopy bed, the soft muted light, all excited his senses and fed his ravenous appetite.

What the hell was wrong with him?

As she brushed past him to lock the door, he covered her hand with his own, trying his best to dismiss the fire coursing through his veins.

"There is no need to lock the door tonight," he said, dropping his hand before he did something he would regret.

"If you're sure."

He simply nodded, fearing his voice would reveal the depth of his desire and so feigned interest in the oak furnishings, in the view from the window, in anything to help cool his heated blood.

"These are an unusual choice," he finally said, pulling the black shutters closed. They felt cold to the touch, the wood moist, and he could smell a faint hint of soil.

"They were not my choice," she replied. "The wind rattles the window at night, and they serve to enhance the sound."

"I imagine the noise is rather like an echo." He turned to face her, pulled his watch from his pocket and squinted to check the time. "Soon it will be midnight. Perhaps we should take our positions."

The corners of her mouth curved up, the weak smile revealing nerves, apprehension. He wasn't sure. "Where do you want me?" she whispered.

Oh, he could answer that question. He wanted her everywhere and every way he possibly could.

"Follow your usual routine." He coughed into his fist, resisted the urge to bite down on his knuckles. "As I said, you do not need to get undressed. I shall pull the chair up to the bed and sit here."

Picking up the chair from the corner of the room, he positioned it in such a way as to offer a perfect view of the door, before hanging his coat over the back and taking a seat.

"Normally, I undress and then wash here," she said, pouring water from a pitcher into a floral bowl. She set about washing her hands, rolling the soap between her elegant fingers, and a waft of lavender drifted through the air just to tease him. She was still wearing her muslin dress, but that was not the vision he saw. "Then I lock the door," she continued as she dried her hands, "fasten the key around my neck and climb into bed."

"And the candles?"

Dipping the tips of her fingers into the water, she extinguished the single candle. The wick sizzled in protest and she tiptoed over to the bed.

Noticing his questioning brow, she added, "Usually, I would have bare feet."

"I see." He turned to inspect the sudden breeze blowing in through the shutters. Thankfully, it had no effect on him as his body was about ready to combust.

After dousing all the candles, they were plunged into darkness, and his other senses soon sprang to attention.

As she lay on the bed, her breathing became short, strained, perhaps from the anticipation of what the next hour would bring. His nose twitched, causing him to inhale deeply. The smell of lavender swamped him now, obliterating the sterile smell that always accompanied the cold.

Even in the dark, he was aware of the rise and fall of her chest. The movement roused thoughts of gentle waves drifting back and forth upon the shore, and he found the image calming, soothing.

They remained silent for a few minutes, maybe more.

Alert to all sounds, Gabriel heard a distinct shuffling noise coming from the room beneath them. Not the shuffling of feet, more like someone pushing an object along a bare floor.

"Did you hear that?" she whispered.

He raised his hand although doubted she could see it in the gloom. "Yes, but I need you to be quiet."

The noise continued for a few minutes and then stopped. It was replaced by a scratching—nails against hollow wood— the sound of someone or something trying to claw its way out of a box.

He was aware of Miss Linwood's hand gripping the counterpane, gathering the material into a tight fist. Guilt delivered a single stab to his chest, a punishment for thinking her foolish and delusional. The terrifying image of her lying night after night alone in her bed delivered the second blow.

How on earth had she coped with this for more than a week?

It was while he was straining to listen that the wind rattled the shutters. The shock made him jump. "Is that a coincidence?" he whispered.

"No. Listen for the weeping."

The sound of squeaking rats could easily be mistaken for

whimpering. Hearing the faint mumble, deeper in tone than a whisper, he closed his eyes to focus his attention. As the noise grew louder, it sounded more like a sorrowful wail. Yet it struck him that it had a distinct pattern, a rhythmical beat, like the chanting of a spell or a curse.

Miss Linwood sat up. "Do you hear it, Mr. Stone?"

"I do," he said, taking a firm hold of his boot before yanking it off and placing it gently on the floor next to him.

"What are you doing?"

"Hush. Taking off my boots," he said, removing the other article in question.

She shuffled closer. "Why?"

"I'm going down there."

Her hand flew out and grabbed his arm, gripping his skin through the fine lawn shirt. "No. You mustn't."

He placed his hand over hers, ignoring the intimacy of the moment. "Lock the door when I'm gone."

With the stealth of a wildcat out on the hunt, Gabriel padded over to the door. Picking up the candlestick on his way out, he held it at his side like a club.

The hallway was dark, but his eyes were accustomed to it now, and with ease he found himself in the Egyptian museum. Glancing up at the ceiling, he imagined the layout of the upstairs rooms and so followed the walkway, searching for the room directly beneath her bedchamber.

As he approached Miss Linwood's office, he could hear the mumbling and followed it to a closed door a few feet away.

This was no curse, he thought, gripping the candlestick tightly, the metal getting hotter in his sweaty palm. This was not an infestation of rats, either.

What he suspected was something far more sinister.

CHAPTER 6

*R*ebecca watched him walk out of the door, her heart beating so hard she thought it might burst through her chest.

Her fear had nothing to do with her own predicament. The only thing she feared now was for the safety of Gabriel Stone.

It should have felt awkward having him in her private chamber. It should have felt unnatural and constrained, but it didn't. For some strange reason, it felt as normal as taking a breath. There was something about his presence that made her feel safe, made her feel the world was full of bright and wonderful things. Now he'd gone, the room felt cold and desolate once more.

She climbed out of bed and tiptoed towards the door. Her head told her to turn the key in the lock. Her heart refused to shut him out.

What if there really was a curse?

What if another bust toppled over the stairs? He would never see it falling in the dark. Mr. Dempsey almost died. Now Gabriel Stone had run off into the night with nothing to aid him but a candlestick.

She knew then what she must do.

Easing the door away from its jamb, she crept out into the hallway, along the corridor and down the stairs.

"Mr. Stone." Rebecca whispered his name.

Her plea was met with nothing but an eerie silence and so she made her way through the Egyptian room, peeking behind the tall display cases as she moved cautiously along. The door at the end of the gallery led out into a hall containing various rooms: her office, the pot room and the storeroom. It was from there that she heard the commotion.

"What the hell!" Mr. Stone yelled at the top of his voice. "Come here, you—"

Loud bangs and thuds were accompanied by the sound of shattering glass and tumbling boxes. She hurried over to the door to grab the handle but it flew open, a frantic figure knocking her to the floor as he took flight along the gallery.

A scream got lost in her throat, and she rolled onto her back to see Gabriel Stone charge at her, his face twisted and contorted, his eyes as cold and as hard as flint. It was as though he didn't know her, seeing only an image of his own creation. He raised the candlestick above his head, and then Rebecca screamed.

"Miss Linwood?" he gasped, his bewildered gaze flitting between her limp body and the figure in the distance. He threw the candlestick to the floor and pulled her back up to her feet. "Are you all right? Are you hurt? Wait here a moment."

He rushed from the room, skidding on the floor as he navigated the door. Barely a minute passed before he returned, his face flushed, his breathing ragged. "He's gone … gone out through the front door."

Rebecca watched him catch his breath, fixated by the raw masculine power emanating from him. His muscular arms strained against the confines of his shirt. His clenched fists were like weapons primed for attack.

"What happened?" she asked. But he ignored her question.

"I told you to lock the door," he said, marching towards her. "What are you doing down here? I almost hit you with the blasted candlestick."

Rebecca took a few deep breaths. "I was worried. I thought something might have happened to you."

He narrowed his gaze and then his expression softened. "You were worried about me?"

When she nodded, he seemed surprised and simply stared at her. "Come," he finally said. "We need to secure the house, and I do not want to leave you up here alone."

Although his words were softer now, he took her by the arm as a parent would a disobedient child.

That was not how she wanted him to see her.

It was not how she wanted him to remember her when he was lying in his bed at night. The thought roused a strange mix of emotions: the need for him to see her as strong and independent and the need for him to see her as a desirable woman.

"Mr. Stone. I am quite capable of walking on my own." She shook her arm free and marched on ahead.

"You may walk on your own, Miss Linwood," he said, catching up with her and turning to block her path. "But you're not spending another night on your own in this house."

The image of her half-brother flashed through her mind. George's need to control outweighed any other good deed. George would have her out of this house, too, if he had his way. He would have her married and settled in the country, away from Society's prying eyes, hidden away from his real family.

"I am not leaving this house, Mr. Stone." She squared her shoulders.

Nothing would sway her decision.

He took a step closer, towering above her, his broad chest casting everything else into shadow. "You will do as I say. And stop calling me Mr. Stone."

Rebecca thrust her hands on her hips, her mind filled with a loathing for all men who sought to rob her of her free will.

"What would you have me call you—Papa? My father is dead, Mr. Stone. I do not need a replacement."

He muttered a curse. "I am trying to help you, or have you forgotten that a man has been lurking in your storeroom for over a week?" He stabbed his finger towards the offending room as though parrying with a sword, each thrust more menacing than the last.

"And I thank you for your help, sir, but you've fulfilled your pledge to me, to my father or to whatever contrived notion of honour you managed to concoct."

He jerked his head back as though her words were a hard punch delivered to weaken his stubborn stance.

"As you rightly said, there is no curse," she continued, determined to show him she was in control, "and so now I shall deal with the matter myself."

He made an odd puffing sound. "Do you think me the sort of man to walk away?"

Something sparked and crackled in the air between them: an undefinable force that excited the senses. Her thoughts shifted to those strong arms, to those soft, full lips, and she tried to find the strength to condemn her traitorous mind to the gallows.

"You're the sort of man who leaves a lady to sit outside on your steps. You're the sort of man who takes pleasure in exerting control, the sort of man happy to call a lady a liar and a thief." Rebecca regretted the words as soon as they'd left her lips, but she could not reclaim them.

His dark brows arched mischievously. "I should be offended." His deep voice sent a ripple of awareness right through her. "Indeed, I am offended. If that is your assessment of my character, perhaps I should add another transgression to the list."

As soon as he moistened his lips, she knew what he was going to do.

"If you're thinking of kissing me, then do it, Mr. Stone." Her tone was strong and firm as she laid down the challenge while her mind was a wreck of fragmented thoughts scattered about a desolate shore.

"Gabriel," he whispered as he lowered his head. "My name is Gabriel."

Just one taste, he thought, just once, just to satisfy the craving burning inside.

It took every ounce of control he had not to ravage her mouth. But he wanted to prolong this moment, wanted to see if it was everything he imagined it to be.

He brushed her lips gently at first, a slow melding of mouths that held a wealth of promise. She did not pull away, and although she lacked experience in such matters, she met him with equal curiosity.

When his hand drifted up to caress her nape, the first pretty sigh left her lips. And then he was lost. His tongue traced the line where her lips met. She let him into her warm, wet mouth, let him coax and tease. The need to taste her, to possess her, to sate this craving, caused his desire to spiral. He almost growled when her untutored tongue met his with a need that matched his own.

His fingers drifted down from her nape, down the curve of her back and he pulled her to his chest. The feel of her soft breasts pressed against him stoked the fire raging within. Then he lost focus as he was carried along on a wave of lustful passion, their tongues lost in each other's mouths, his manhood hard and throbbing with need.

It was as though she had a magical ability to be everywhere all at once. The smell of lavender filled his head as did some other exotic scent specific to her. He could taste claret. He could hear her little pants and moans, and he wanted to lay her down and drive into her over and over again until she clawed at his shoulders and cried out his name.

"*Gabriel.*"

It took him a moment to realise she had whispered his name, the sound caressing his needy body like featherlight fingers. His hands moved lower, cupping her as he lifted her off her feet, pushing her back against the display cabinet.

"Mr. Stone. The … the antiquities."

It was as though she had thrown a bucket of ice-cold water over him, forcing him to open his eyes, to drag his mouth from hers.

"Miss Linwood," he panted, as his mind tried to assemble what had just happened. He lowered her down until her feet touched the floor and brushed the loose strands of hair off her face.

They stood there, staring into each other's eyes, their ragged breathing the only audible sound.

He waited for the lump to form in his throat, for a pang of guilt to stab away at his chest, but it did not come. He wondered if he should ask for forgiveness, but he was not sorry. Watching her put her fingers to her swollen lips made him want to kiss her again.

"Do you want to pretend that didn't happen?" he said.

In one respect, it would be easier if she said yes. It would be easier to forget how sweet she tasted, to forget she was able to penetrate the wall he'd erected. But the reality was, he would never forget how good it felt to hold her in his arms.

"Do you?" she asked, her vivid green eyes fixated on his mouth.

A smile threatened to form on his lips. "I believe I asked first."

She shrugged, and he could sense her inner torment as he suspected it mirrored his own. Perhaps honesty was the best way forward.

"No, I don't want to pretend. And I am not sorry," he said, his abdomen tightening when he looked at her flushed cheeks and mussed hair. "But it was a moment of madness where I forgot my manners and my sense of honour, even if it is contrived."

"About that," she said, looking down at the floor. "I did not mean what I said earlier. I did not mean—"

"It doesn't matter now," he interrupted. "Besides, I must make allowances for your fragile state." When he noticed the muscle in her jaw twitch, he added, "Upon finding an intruder in your home."

He was wrong to imply that the man hiding in the store-room had an interest in the house. Whoever he was, he was only interested in frightening Miss Linwood.

"Do you know what he was doing in there?"

Gabriel shook his head. "He was hiding behind some

boxes and waited for me to walk inside before darting for the door."

"I shall speak to Mr. Pearce in the morning. Perhaps he has noticed something untoward."

"Mr. Pearce?"

"My curator."

Gabriel resisted the urge to tell her not to talk to anyone, not without him being present. Perhaps she was right. He was starting to think like an overbearing parent. Why did he even care? He brushed his hand through his hair in an attempt to banish the feeling that, somehow, she had found a way through his barrier. He could still taste her on his lips, still smell the heady scent of her desire, still feel her soft, pliant body pressed against his.

"Perhaps we could talk to Mr. Pearce together," he suggested. "I cannot walk away until I have dealt with the matter here."

And I must walk away, he added silently, *as I could never be the man you would want me to be.*

"I understand." She nodded. "You may call before luncheon tomorrow."

"You mistake my intention," he said firmly, amazed she would even consider going up to her room on her own after what had just happened. "I will not leave you here alone. I can stay, or you can come with me. I'm open to suggestions and will do whatever you think appropriate." Just to reinforce his point, he added, "If you refuse, I shall be forced to sleep outside your front door."

Without a word, she turned away from him and paced back and forth, her head bowed. Using her thumb and forefinger, she pulled gently on her lips. "And you will assist me only until the intruder is caught?" she said, swinging around to face him.

Gabriel offered a bow. "I will assist you until I am satisfied you're safe."

Perhaps he should call upon her brothers and see if they could take her in.

Miss Linwood folded her arms across her chest. "But you cannot stay here. People will talk. And I'm not leaving."

"No one knows I'm here." Only the members of his staff would know he had not come home. But they were used to him trailing about to odd places at short notice. "If I remain in your quarters, for this evening at least, then I shall be able to make an assessment of the storeroom in the morning. With any luck, the matter will be concluded by tomorrow evening."

Indeed, he would begin by making a thorough investigation of the curator, Mr. Pearce.

"Where would you sleep?"

Gabriel pursed his lips to suppress a grin, imagining her shocked expression if he told her he would share her bed. "I recall seeing a chaise. I shall be fine on there. If you would be so good as to find me a blanket."

Her gaze drifted over him, lingering on his stocking feet, before advancing up over his chest and mouth. "Very well. But we shall review the terms on a daily basis."

Gabriel nodded. "Agreed. I shall need to go and secure the rooms downstairs."

"I shall go and find a blanket."

They walked in opposite directions. But when he glanced over his shoulder, he caught her looking back at him. "I shall meet you upstairs," he said.

Once confident all the doors were locked, he made his way back upstairs and found Miss Linwood sitting on the chaise, clutching a pillow and blanket.

"Will you be warm enough?" she asked as she stood and offered him the items before retreating towards the door.

"I will be fine. Oh, and please lock your door, Miss Linwood."

Her hands flew up to her chest. "Why? Do you think the intruder will return?"

Gabriel sighed. "No. It's not the intruder I'm worried about."

CHAPTER 7

*T*he thin streams of light shooting through the gaps in the shutters pricked at Rebecca's eyes, rousing her from a peaceful slumber. With a stretch and a yawn, she raised herself up on her elbows and surveyed the room. Everything looked the same as it always did.

Yet it felt different—she felt different.

It had taken hours to drift off, her thoughts frolicking in the secret place before sleep and dreams. There, she had waltzed with Gabriel Stone, strolled through meadows and kissed him under the stars. She relived the moment his lips first met hers, the way his hot mouth robbed her of her breath, the way her mind and body melted into liquid fire when held in his arms.

In this private realm, she was free to indulge in lascivious thoughts. Her cheeks flamed at the memory of his aroused body pressed against her. Desire coursed through her veins like a delicious form of agony.

She should have been ashamed of those feelings. But how could she? They made her feel alive and free. They made her forget she was all alone in the world?

Gabriel Stone drifted into her thoughts as she washed, as her fingers followed the outline of her lips. When she brushed her hair, she thought she could smell the woody aroma that clung to his skin. When she smoothed the creases from her brown dress, her stomach grew warm as she recalled the way his gaze had followed the outline of her breasts.

Rebecca sighed and shook her head, as though the action would wake the logical part of her brain, the part still sleepy and dormant.

When she was ready, she sauntered into the room, expecting to see Mr. Stone up and dressed, too. But he was fast asleep; his large frame squashed on the narrow chaise. The blanket clung to his arms and had bunched up around his torso, leaving his bare feet poking out of the bottom.

She needed to wake him, but he looked so peaceful and content.

The soft rhythmical sound of his breathing was like food for the soul and her thoughts moved away from the initial tug of desire. Instead, she imagined crawling up between those muscular arms and sleeping, too.

Perhaps somewhere in his subconscious he became aware of her standing there staring at him. Indeed, he stretched his arms above his head and gave a satisfied hum.

In a panic, she scurried over to the table and tried to stop her heart from thumping against her ribs. She busied about, clearing last nights plates, putting the decanter back on its tray in the hope the tinkering would alert him to her presence.

"Forgive me," he suddenly said, his voice drifting across the room, the husky tones of sleep massaging her senses. "I do not usually sleep so late."

When Rebecca turned to face him, she swallowed.

He was sitting up, his elbows resting on his knees as he brushed his hands through his hair to tame the unruly black locks. She noticed his waistcoat and cravat draped over the chair, the whole scene being one of relaxed intimacy.

An intimacy shared by lovers.

"It is only s-seven," she stuttered, failing in her attempt to look anywhere in the room except at him.

He groaned as he drew the palm of his hand down his face.

"I will leave you to dress," she added, desperate to get all her words out before she choked on them. "You may use my room to wash. There's fresh water in the pitcher. I shall go downstairs and prepare something to eat. Do you drink coffee, Mr. Stone?"

"Gabriel," he said with a mischievous grin, "and yes, Miss Linwood, I drink coffee."

"Excellent." She beamed as she collected a handful of plates. The delicate china clattered together as she could not stop her hands from shaking.

"Would you like some help?"

She swung around, and a knife went skittering across the floor. "No, I will be perfectly fine." But he ignored her comment and walked over to pick it up.

As he placed it back on top of the plates, her gaze betrayed her inner thoughts, as it refused to move from the dusting of dark hair peeking out from beneath the open collar of his shirt.

A smile played on his lips. "I should get dressed."

Rebecca spent twenty minutes preparing ham, eggs and toast. Her thoughts flitted between giving Mr. Stone time to wash and dress and rushing to finish before Mrs. James came back at eight.

She walked back into the room to find him admiring the painting of her mother, his clothing as impeccable as when he'd first arrived. Upon hearing the rattling tray, he rushed over, took it from her and carried it to the table, and they began their meal in comfortable silence.

"I was wondering why you didn't seek the help of your brothers when you suspected you were cursed. Your father had three sons. Surely one of them took an interest in his work."

Taking a sip of his coffee he watched her over the rim of his cup, his brow arched while waiting for her reply. What was she supposed to say? They despised her. They despised their father. She would make a pact with Satan before asking for their help.

"They are not my brothers, Mr. Stone," she corrected stiffly. "They are my father's sons."

He stared at her with those hungry eyes of his, and she became conscious of the way she was eating, sitting and breathing—each one of the simple tasks feeling awkward and new.

"Is there a difference?" he asked.

She put down her cutlery and dabbed her lips with a napkin. "Do you honestly need me to answer that?" When he shrugged, she said, "They were not happy about their father's relationship with my mother. They are not happy I have this house and are not happy I exist at all."

The answer seemed to unsettle him. Lost in his own thoughts, his eyes glazed as though recalling a distant memory, one painful and unwelcome.

"Well, that explains a great deal," he finally said. "I wondered why you sought me out."

The reason had nothing to do with the inadequacy of her half-brothers and everything to do with his ability to accomplish the task.

"When it comes to the study of the ancient world, I could think of no man better qualified."

He inclined his head to acknowledge the compliment.

"Talking of which," Rebecca continued, "perhaps we should make our way downstairs. It would not be prudent to let Mrs. James discover us eating breakfast together."

"Or discover that I slept the night." He gave a devilish grin as he walked around the table to hold out her chair. "Do you have the list I asked for?"

"Yes. It's on my desk."

"Come, let us hurry downstairs to your office," he said, picking up his plate. "I shall hide this in the kitchen. It would not do to have someone stumble upon our secret rendezvous."

Standing in her office, Mr. Stone scanned the list, his lips moving as he read her notes. Rebecca stood and watched, remembering the way they'd moved so expertly over her mouth.

"So, the only person with a key to the premises is Mr. Pearce. Is it wise to give him unrestricted access? After all, your private apartments are in this house."

"He is the curator, Mr. Stone. Of course he needs access."

In truth, his words of caution left her feeling a little cold. She had never even considered the possibility that one of her staff would enter the house without warrant.

"Then perhaps you should look for somewhere else to live."

Oh, this gentleman knew how to aggravate her temper. "I cannot afford to live anywhere else." She braced her hands on her hips. "And I cannot leave the museum unattended."

"If money is the issue, have you considered marriage?"

Had his words not presented a perfect opportunity to tease him, she would have stamped on his toe. "Mr. Stone, how wonderful of you to offer." She fluttered her lashes. "Rebecca Stone has a certain elegance about it, don't you think?"

"I was not referring to myself," he said, glancing back at

the notes. "Although now I have witnessed you performing your daily ablutions, perhaps it is only right I do make you an offer."

With wide eyes and a trembling lip, her gaze met his. "Well ... well, I do not want a husband. I could not tolerate any man telling me what to do." When she noticed he was pursing his lips to suppress a chuckle, she batted him on the arm. "You're teasing me, aren't you?"

He laughed then, his eyes sparkling with genuine amusement. "I am. But only because you saw fit to do the same."

His laughter was infectious, and she laughed, too. "So, I take it you don't like the sound of Rebecca Stone?"

"I think Rebecca is a fine name. Indeed, as the Bible reminds us, Rebecca was kind and generous by nature." His gaze fell to her mouth before drifting up to her hair. "She was extremely beautiful."

He was teasing her again.

"But she married a man more than twice her age."

"Yes, but he truly loved her. Is that not what is important? Is that not what you wish for yourself?"

A hard lump formed in her throat. The words were another reminder she was alone in the world. No one cared for her, and it didn't matter how many times she swallowed, it would not go away.

"I am not the sort to indulge in whimsical fantasies, Mr. Stone," she said, aware her voice sounded strained.

"Yet another thing we seem to have in common."

Why did he persist in saying things that made her body react in a multitude of different ways? One minute she felt as though she had a stone tablet stuck in her throat, the next her stomach was overrun with an infestation of butterflies. It wasn't just what he said. It was the way the words fell from his lips, the rich drawl that teased and stroked her senses.

"I think we seem to have drifted from the point," she said, mentally shaking herself. "As my curator, I must assume that Mr. Pearce is innocent of any wrongdoing until such a time he proves otherwise."

He placed the list on her desk. When their eyes met, his arched brow suggested she was extremely naive. "In my book, it is always best to assume a person is guilty until they prove otherwise."

Rebecca could not help but wonder what had happened in his life for him to have such a cynical view of the world. Indeed, cynicism was a principle he applied to most things, including love and marriage.

"Well, in some things we are different." She sighed. "Shall we see what damage he's done to the storeroom?"

He nodded and waved his hand for her to lead the way.

The storeroom door was still open. Various boxes and crates were scattered about the floor. The untidy spectacle caused her to draw a deep breath.

Gabriel put his arm out to prevent her from dashing in. "Mind where you walk. There is glass on the floor from the cabinet." He pointed to the display case on the far wall. "It is my fault. I swung the candlestick at the intruder but misjudged the space. I shall pay to have it replaced."

"It doesn't matter. Besides, you have done more than enough to compensate." Only when he raised a sinful brow was she aware of what she'd said. "I was referring to your help with the intruder."

"Oh, there's no need to be shy, Miss Linwood. It's gratifying to know one's efforts have not gone unnoticed."

Rebecca rolled her eyes. "I shall go and find a broom."

When she returned, he was busy inspecting the room, rummaging around in crates and moving boxes and so she brushed the floor to clear a walkway.

"You know, you should have this on display." He removed a bronze spoon from a box. "It's Eighteenth Dynasty. I have yet to see a finer specimen."

"Put it back. I know where everything is, or at least I did."

He put it back in the box and covered it with straw. "Then you should look around to see if anything is missing. Perhaps theft was the motive. Perhaps the culprit hoped the noises would prevent you from venturing down here."

"I think you forget, the noises started after I read from the scroll," she said, propping the broom up against the wall before opening one of the boxes. "Are you not the least bit intrigued to see what it says?"

"No. Not yet. We have already established there is no such thing as a curse. Someone is doing their utmost to scare you. The operative word being *someone* and not *something*." He glanced up at the ceiling and then moved to stand at the side of the cabinet. "Step back a few paces."

Rebecca obeyed his command.

"But it cannot all be a coincidence. I mean, there is the matter of the bed shaking and the wind rattling my shutters. Why are you moving the cabinet?"

He peered behind the tall wooden structure and then plastered his body flat against the wall, stretching his hand behind until his arm disappeared from view. "There is something hanging from the wall," he said. "It's probably nothing, but— wait a moment—it's a rope."

The sound of her bed creaking above stairs caught Rebecca's attention. "Did you hear that? The noise is coming from my room."

"Would you mind passing me the broom?"

Rebecca handed him the broom, his fingers brushing against hers as he grasped the handle. She watched him poke at the ceiling, heard a crack as the plaster crumbled away.

"The rope goes up through a hole in the ceiling." He withdrew his arm and brushed the dust from his coat sleeve. "We should go upstairs and inspect your room."

The thought of being alone with him again in such a private space caused her stomach to lurch. "Let us be quick about it then, before someone sees us."

When they entered her room, he walked over to her bed. "I will need you to help me pull it away from the wall."

His words and movements were structured and methodical, and she did not think to question his motive. Together, they gripped the bottom of the bed and pulled it back a few inches.

"That should be sufficient." He moved the side table to get a better view. "It is as I suspected. The rope's attached to the frame of your bed."

He straightened and strode over to the window, scanning the square panes until he found what he was looking for. "And a pane of glass is missing from the corner of this window."

She moved towards him, her breathing shallow as she stared up at rows upon rows of tiny squares, aware of the light breeze drifting through.

"Who would do such a thing?"

"If the intention is to cause harm, then the intruder has had every opportunity to succeed in his task. This is different. Someone is trying to frighten you, so you must try to think why anyone would wish to cause you distress."

Rebecca hung her head. Her chest felt hollow. Beneath her ribcage there was nothing but an empty cavern. Mr. Stone took hold of her chin and lifted her head until her eyes met his.

"I promise you, I will find out who is doing this and put

an end to the nightmare." He pressed his lips to her forehead before straightening.

The small gesture, the kiss that spoke of comfort and compassion, was worth more to her than any jewel or ancient relic.

It meant more to her than he would ever know.

CHAPTER 8

*S*eeing the coarse rope attached to the bed, seeing the look of horror on Miss Linwood's face caused something to snap inside Gabriel's chest.

He would find the person responsible and then there would be hell to pay.

Even as they made their way down to her office, he could still see the look of fear in her eyes. As much as she tried to make others believe she was strong and resilient, there was a certain vulnerability about her that called out to him.

The different aspects of her character were like the facets of a gem: each unique angle contributing to its dazzling beauty. As the owner of the museum, she was forthright, haughty and knowledgeable, and he enjoyed their discussions about the ancient world.

Then, there was another side. A fragility that roused a medieval sense of chivalry, something he had forgotten he possessed. Perhaps the most intriguing aspect of all was the fiery passion simmering beneath the surface. He had only glimpsed it, only sipped the sweet nectar from a cup he imagined was as deep as the ocean.

"Are you well, Mr. Stone?"

Her voice penetrated his thoughts, and he realised they were standing in the middle of the gallery. "Yes, Miss Linwood. Forgive me. I was just thinking about the intruder."

She stepped closer and lowered her voice. "Well, perhaps we can cross Mr. Pearce off the list. Look, he has made an appearance this morning."

Miss Linwood's naivety touched him.

He followed her gaze to one of the display cabinets, to the painfully thin gentleman whose bony fingers were busy scanning the pages of a ledger. It was obvious the man wasn't reading as his eyes moved up and down the page at too rapid a rate.

"I need you to trust me, Miss Linwood." Gabriel placed her hand in the crook of his arm and forced her to follow his direction. "I need you to agree with everything I say, without question or reservation. Regardless of how strange it sounds."

He gave her no chance to protest as he stepped in front of the curator. "Mr. Pearce. Good morning."

The man looked up, his left eye twitching. Gabriel doubted he suffered from an uncontrollable muscle spasm. The curator inclined his head to Miss Linwood and with a stutter said, "G-good morning."

"I am Mr. Stone, Miss Linwood's new partner in the museum."

The absence of a top lip did not prevent the curator's mouth from quivering. "I was not aware that—"

"I asked Miss Linwood to refrain from discussing the matter," Gabriel interrupted, "as we had not agreed on the details. But rest assured I shall be spending a ridiculous amount of time here."

Gabriel glanced at Miss Linwood, his eyes darting to the right to inform her it was her turn to speak.

"You must understand," she began, "I could not discuss the matter until I was certain of Mr. Stone's intentions. But he is considered an expert on ancient Egypt and his knowledge will be invaluable to us."

Although he had told her to agree with him, he rather liked that she held him in such high regard.

"I have antiquities of my own that I intend to display," Gabriel added with an exaggerated wave of the hand. "I thought you could accompany us to the office to discuss the best way to proceed."

The mere mention of his own objects caused an odd feeling to form in his stomach. The feeling he imagined one would get when conducting an illicit affair: the thrill and anticipation of a passionate encounter waging a bitter battle with a moral responsibility. He dismissed the image of his lonely books left abandoned on his desk, deserted and forsaken. After all, he was not betraying them; he was in a museum filled with the wonders of Egypt. Perhaps he would stumble upon something to further his knowledge on the process of mummification.

Gabriel waved his hand, instructing Mr. Pearce to take the lead. "On you go, Mr. Pearce. We shall follow."

The gentleman edged past them and skulked off towards the office, glancing behind periodically, as though aware of Gabriel's piercing gaze burrowing into his back.

Once in the room, Miss Linwood took her place behind the desk and invited Mr. Pearce to sit opposite. Gabriel stood, knowing his pacing would unnerve the curator.

"There is also another matter that needs addressing," Gabriel said, slamming the office door to make Mr. Pearce jump. "And it relates to my reservations regarding the security of my own objects."

"I can assure you," Mr. Pearce said, his head moving left

and right while he tried to locate Gabriel, "we treat all the antiquities with extreme care."

"But that is not the case, is it, Mr. Pearce?" Gabriel moved to the curator's side. "You see, for the past week, someone has been sneaking into the storeroom at night. The antiquities are in disarray, boxes open and scattered across the floor and yet you have said nothing to Miss Linwood. Why is that?"

Gabriel glanced at Miss Linwood, whose expression resembled someone on the front row of a gladiatorial arena, waiting to see if the outcome would be thumbs up or down.

"I—I've not been in the storeroom," Pearce stammered.

Gabriel moved to stand next to Miss Linwood. He folded his arms across his chest and frowned. "A curator of a museum has not been in his storeroom or taken an inventory of its treasures for a whole week?" He feigned amazement. "Is this how you normally work, Miss Linwood?"

"No. Not at all. The list should be checked daily, Mr. Stone."

Mr. Pearce ran his fingers along the edge of his collar and craned his neck as though his shirt chafed his skin. He looked at Miss Linwood, then at Gabriel, before turning to look at the closed door.

"Well, the constable will tell us more when we have assessed the damage. Of course, he will want to look at the item the intruder dropped, and I will conduct a meeting with all staff. The motive is obviously theft." He turned to Miss Linwood. "What did you say was missing?"

Her eyes widened and then she said, "The bronze spoon is missing from its box. It is Eighteenth Dynasty."

"Add that to trespass," Gabriel said, counting the list of transgressions on his fingers, "damage to property and intention to cause bodily harm. Once we find the person responsible, I'm certain he'll hang."

"It is not my fault," Mr. Pearce cried, jumping up from his chair. "You cannot blame a man for doing what he is told. It was his lordship. He made me do it. But I swear to you, I have stolen nothing."

Gabriel sensed Miss Linwood's body stiffen. It was always unpleasant to discover one's trust had been misplaced. In his head, he imagined putting a comforting hand on her shoulder to ease the tension, which would probably have stopped her from jumping out of her chair, too.

"You mean to tell me it … it was George Wellford who asked you to break into my home in the dead of night and scare me out of my wits?" She leant over the desk, her face level with Mr. Pearce.

The curator could only stare at the floor.

"Of all the sneaky, underhanded … ugh … you may tell Lord Wellford to go to the devil." She swung around to face Gabriel. "What did I tell you? He wants me out of here and will do whatever it takes to achieve his goal."

Gabriel waved his hands up and down: a simple gesture to calm a volatile spirit. "Let us hear what Mr. Pearce has to say on the matter," he said, turning to face the gentleman. "What precisely did Lord Wellford ask you to do?"

Mr. Pearce held his hands in front of him and fiddled with his fingers. "I was to frighten her a little. That is all. Lord Wellford wants Miss Linwood to understand that the museum is no place for an unmarried lady."

"You see, he wants me out of London," she said. "Trust me, he will have a gentleman with a purse full of coins ready and waiting to cart me off to the country."

The image of Miss Linwood as the wife of a country squire

did not sit well with Gabriel. He could not imagine her taking tea with the vicar or hosting a summer fete or being out in the garden pruning roses. The lady had a passionate spirit and a deep love of the ancient world. It would be like trying to contain a butterfly in a jar. Eventually, her spirit would wither and fade. Her father would not have left her the house and all his treasures if he had not thought her capable. If she were to marry, then the gentleman would have to accept that the museum was her life, and he doubted there were many men willing to do so.

"You were never in any danger," Mr. Pearce said, finding the courage to look up at the lady. "I acted out of concern, nothing more."

"Concern!" she spat. "You need not concern yourself with me."

"Did Lord Wellford pay you?" Gabriel said.

Mr. Pearce nodded and scrunched up his face as though the words forming in his mouth were painful. "He … he gave me ten pounds."

Miss Linwood threw her hands up in the air. "Ten pounds! Is that the price of a lady's sanity?"

"I have a family. What was I supposed to do?"

Gabriel gritted his teeth. "You were supposed to act honourably out of respect for your patron. Am I to understand Wellford gave you the ancient scroll?"

Mr. Pearce nodded. "He said it was a copy of an old curse. He said Miss Linwood would be more inclined to believe it."

"Right," Miss Linwood said, banging her hands on the desk. "Mr. Pearce. You will go to the storeroom and clear up the mess. With your ten pounds, I suggest you pay for someone to come and fix the hole in my ceiling. That is if you wish to continue working here."

Gabriel gaped in astonishment. "You're not letting him stay?"

"I shall decide his fate when I have spoken to Lord Wellford. Now, be on your way, Mr. Pearce, before I change my mind."

The man scurried from the room as though wolves were biting at his heels.

"Surely you're not going to let him stay," Gabriel repeated, as he was struggling to believe how anyone could be so lenient. He wanted to thrust his fist down the man's throat in the hope of pulling out his missing lip.

"I do not mind saying this to you, Mr. Stone, but my head is in such a tizzy I am not sure what is going on." She flopped back down into the chair and let out a deep sigh. "I thank you for all your help. You must think me rather foolish for believing in a curse."

"On the contrary," he said. "When I first heard the noises, I was tempted to believe it myself. Had the scroll been written in another language, then I'm sure I would have been more inclined to agree with you."

It was not a lie. Well, perhaps it was a small exaggeration.

"Talking of the scroll, I had best go and remove it from the crate. I intend to feed it to Lord Wellford for luncheon in the hope he chokes." She smiled at him, and the world seemed suddenly brighter. "I'm sure you will be relieved to get back to your studies now the matter is resolved. I have wasted far too much of your time."

Gabriel waited to feel the burning in his chest, the craving that tugged at his stomach whenever he thought of his work. But for some reason, it did not come. Perhaps his mind was so preoccupied with this tempting beauty he had lost sight of what was important. The only way to correct that was to immerse himself in his books.

Which was why he was somewhat shocked when he said, "I will come with you when you visit Lord Wellford. It would not hurt to let him believe we are partners, at least for the time being."

Her eyes widened. "I could not ask you to do that," she said, although a look of relief flashed across her face.

"But only if you think I may be of some use," he added, in the hope of appeasing the independent side of her character. "I said I would help you until the matter is concluded and I am a man of my word."

"Well, at least if you're there, then there is no chance of him locking me in his cellar while he hurries off to summon a suitor."

Gabriel glanced down at his dusty coat. "I will need to change out of these clothes and shall return with my carriage."

"You have a carriage?" she said with some surprise.

"My father was the youngest son of a viscount. Consequently, I have money, but no title."

Miss Linwood looked up at him as though he had sprouted horns. "How wonderful. So, presumably, you have an uncle or a cousin who is a viscount."

"An uncle." He nodded, but recalled only seeing him once since his father's death.

"So when you say you are on your own, you mean you have no siblings," she clarified.

Gabriel swallowed to clear the lump from his throat.

"Like you, I do have family to speak of." He chose not to answer her question directly as he did not want to lie to her. "But I prefer to be alone."

CHAPTER 9

"*Y*ou're certain Lord Wellford will see you?" Mr. Stone said as the carriage rattled along Compton Street on its way to Bedford Square.

Sitting in such close quarters, Rebecca struggled to breathe let alone rouse a coherent response.

He sat opposite, his muscular thighs straining against pale buckskin breeches. Their knees were but an inch apart and despite the bumps and rumbles, he maintained the distance.

It was odd how she craved his company.

She should have told him she could deal with George on her own. But for some strange reason, the thought of being near him for a few more hours seemed far too tempting to resist. Even now, in the dark confines of his carriage, the air pulsed with some undefinable emotion: a feeling of need, of longing, of desperation. She could feel the energy sparking between them, heating her blood, and it took all her efforts to focus on the conversation.

"If he refuses to see me, I shall sit outside his front door until he has no choice but to open it." Her gaze drifted over his broad shoulders encased in a dark blue coat, and she imagined bronzed skin stretched smoothly over each bulging contour. "I do not think he is as stubborn as you, Mr. Stone."

His eyes glinted with mischief, and he did not look the least bit studious. He looked like a devilish rogue.

"So you think me stubborn, Miss Linwood?" He sat forward and the exotic scent of spice and something utterly masculine filled her head. "Do you remember what happened the last time you drew attention to the flaws in my character?"

There was something different about him now. Something so opposed to the man she first met at Lord Banbury's ball. He appeared more relaxed, his voice smooth and warm, his gaze firm and focused. Rebecca could feel the blush rising in her cheeks as she recalled their passionate encounter. Under such scrutiny, a lady should look to her lap to convey her modesty. Instead, she found the courage to look him in the eye.

"I shall never forget it, Mr. Stone," she said, a little surprised that her own voice sounded deeper than usual.

He sucked in a breath as his gaze lingered on her lips. When he exhaled slowly, she felt a ripple of pleasure flow through her body and all she could think of was how wonderful it felt to be lost in his sinful mouth.

"Morality is a peculiar thing," he said with a sigh, throwing himself back in his seat. "At times, it feels like a thick iron rod running through me, one that refuses to bend to my will."

Every logical part of her mind told her to ignore his comment, told her to look out of the window and feign interest in anything other than those ravenous brown eyes.

"Are you suggesting you wish to be immoral, Mr. Stone?" She felt a strange thrum of excitement course through her as she waited for his answer.

He looked at her beneath hooded lids. "What do you think, Miss Linwood? Do you think me a gentleman capable of suppressing immoral thoughts?"

"I believe you are a gentleman capable of doing anything you set your mind to."

"Your faith in me is flattering." He covered his heart with his hand. "However, it does not stop me from wanting to do a host of unseemly things."

The fluttering sensation in her stomach rose to her throat. The topic of conversation was immoral, but she was not the least bit offended. On the contrary, it was a testament to their friendship—if that was how one would define their relationship—that he could speak openly and honestly and so she chose to do the same.

"Do you think I do not feel the same temptations, Mr. Stone? Do you think me cold to your heated gaze? Do you think desire only flows through your veins?"

When his open mouth snapped shut, he gave an amused chuckle. "I doubt it is the same," he said with a dismissive shrug.

As a novice to the skill of seduction, she should have been drowning in the depths of her own innocence. Yet she wanted to excite him, to prove she could match him stroke for stroke.

"Well, Mr. Stone. Perhaps one day you may get the opportunity to find out."

With his mouth curved into a lascivious grin, he replied, "Now it is not only my interest that is piqued, Miss Linwood."

The carriage jolted to a halt, and the spell was broken.

Mr. Stone opened the door and jumped to the pavement. "Don't get down, Higson. I shall help Miss Linwood." He did not bother to lower the step and, despite her gasp, wrapped his strong hands around her waist and lifted her down. "Perhaps you are my Achilles' heel, Miss Linwood," he said as she brushed the creases out of her dress. "The more time I spend in your company, the more all respectable intentions are lost."

"Don't lose heart, Mr. Stone. I never said I wanted you to be respectable." Rebecca patted him on the chest before sauntering past to knock on Lord Wellford's door.

Thankfully, she did not have to throw herself across the threshold or bang loudly demanding an audience. Winters, Lord Wellford's butler, instructed them to wait in the hall. After a few minutes, he returned to escort them into the drawing room.

"Lord Wellford will be with you shortly." Winters gave a solemn bow before making a silent retreat.

Rebecca set about untying her bonnet before sitting on the sofa. She nodded to Mr. Stone when he gestured to the space beside her.

"George will wonder why we are here together," she said, rooting around in her reticule in search of the ancient scroll.

"That did occur to me. Perhaps I should be grateful he is not party to my immoral thoughts," he said. When she plucked out the offending article, he asked, "Would you mind if I had a look at that?"

"Of course not. I'm surprised your innate sense of curiosity has not insisted on making a thorough examination."

She handed it to him, and he unwound the tiny piece of paper, muttering the words as he scanned the elegant script.

"Coupled with the strange noises at night, I can see why you thought this might be genuine. *I shall cast fear unto him,*" he read, his voice as emotive as a preacher delivering a sermon to a crowd full of sinners, "*and the wind will howl your sins—*"

"Don't read it!" she cried, making a feeble attempt to grab it out of his hand.

"*And the dead will rise again!*"

"Mr. Stone!"

"I've already told you," he said in a humorous tone. "There is no such thing as a curse. Until recently, we had no way of deciphering hieroglyphics let alone place a more in-depth meaning to them. This scroll is just an attempt to frighten you." He thrust his arm in the air and read some more. "*Let crocodiles chase her through water. Let—*"

"It does not say that." She tried to snatch it from his hand.

The sound of someone clearing his throat caught her attention and Rebecca turned to see George Wellford standing in the doorway.

"Oh, don't mind me," he said as he walked into the room. "One rarely gets the chance to see two people fighting over a piece of paper."

"We were not fighting, my lord," Rebecca said as they both stood to greet him.

With his golden hair and warm smile, she found it almost impossible to be angry with him. Perhaps it was the soft timbre of his voice or his bright blue eyes that made her heart forgive all of his sins. Perhaps that was why she chose not to spend time in his company: out of fear she might grow to like him.

"Rebecca," he said with a respectful bow. "You do not have to greet me so formally. Are we not kin?" When she didn't answer, he looked past her. "Stone. It has been a while."

"Four years, Lord Wellford."

George raised a brow. "Has it been so long? My father, or should I say our father, was extremely fond of you. I think he always hoped I would share your enthusiasm for his work.

But I'm afraid I was a constant disappointment." He glanced briefly at Rebecca. "I hope his faith in you as a gentleman was not misplaced."

"Not at all," Mr. Stone replied. "It is out of respect and concern for Miss Linwood that I have accompanied her here today."

George waved his hand at the sofa. "Then please take a seat. I did not imagine you were here to gossip and drink tea." He waited for them to sit and then sat in the chair opposite, his gaze firm as he steepled his fingers in front of his chest. "But first, I should like to know the nature of your involvement, Mr. Stone."

Rebecca decided to answer on his behalf. "Mr. Stone is my closest friend and my business partner." He was her only friend and her partner in the most sinful kiss of her life. "He intends to display some pieces at the museum."

"Is it wise for an unmarried lady to name a gentleman amongst her friends, Rebecca?" His disapproving gaze drifted back and forth between them.

Rebecca's chest grew tight. If she were a cat, she would hiss, arch her back and splay her claws. Why did George make a simple observation sound like a scathing reprimand?

"Thankfully, I do not have to concern myself with what is considered appropriate," she informed coldly. "As you know, my parents are dead, my lord. So I may choose my friends and my business associates as I please."

"As the daughter of a respected peer, your reputation should be important to you."

The sweeping statement caused her heart to thump against her chest. "I may be the daughter of a peer but I was born out of wedlock, or have you forgotten? Besides, it is hardly an appropriate topic of conversation to have in front of guests."

The room fell silent. The only sound she was aware of was her own ragged breath.

"Miss Linwood came to me because she believed she had brought a dreadful curse upon herself," Mr. Stone finally said. The words sounded measured and controlled, yet Rebecca could feel the tension emanating from him. "She heard voices at night, scratching and moaning while the wind rattled her shutters, and a mysterious force shook her bed. As a lady living alone, you can imagine how terrifying that would be."

George did not even attempt to look shocked or embarrassed but just sat there as though listening to yet another report of the day's weather.

Mr. Stone gritted his teeth. The muscles in his jaw twitched. "The noises were made by an intruder," he continued, "and frightened her out of her wits."

The mere mention of the intruder brought the memory of the haunting flooding back. On the first night, she had thought rats were scurrying about the boxes, thought she had imagined the bed move. It was on the second night that she heard the moaning. She'd imagined a figure floating up the stairs, had held her breath while she waited for it to burst through the door.

"We know it was you," she suddenly blurted, releasing the fear she had held on to for more than a week. "We know you arranged it all."

"I take it Mr. Pearce confessed." George gave a hapless shrug. "What do you want me to say, Rebecca? If you want me to say I'm sorry—I'm not." He ignored Mr. Stone's sudden intake of breath. "You were never in any danger. But it is only a matter of time before something untoward happens to you."

Mr. Stone thrust himself forward. "You're wrong. She was in danger, in danger of losing her sanity. In her desperation, she could have fled the house in the dead of night. Do you know how many unpleasant characters wander the streets at such an ungodly hour?"

His words appeared to have some effect. For the first time, George's cobalt-blue eyes flashed with remorse.

"What else was I to do?" George asked, pushing his hand through his golden locks. "She refuses to heed my advice, insists on calling herself Miss Linwood when it is clearly not the name of her birth. She needs the protection of her family."

No matter what George said, Rebecca would never be a Wellford. He could plead, protest and dress it all up with a fancy ribbon. It would not change the fact she was not part of his family.

Mr. Stone sighed. "What do you want from her?"

"I know what he wants," she said. "He wants to chase me out of my home so he can claim it for himself."

"You know that is not true, Rebecca," George said softly. "What need do I have for a house full of dusty old relics? I want you to accept you have a place here, with your family, that is all." He turned his attention to Mr. Stone. "You have kin. I recall there being a younger sister. Tell me you do not want what is best for her."

Rebecca turned sharply. Why had he not mentioned he had a sister? When her eyes met his, the pain she saw there made her heart ache.

"My sister is only ten years old," he said with a hint of sadness in his voice, "and while I can understand your motives, I cannot condone your methods. Miss Linwood shares your father's passion for the ancient world. Her home is a place filled with magic and wonder. It is a place where she feels connected to her parents."

Rebecca continued to stare at him. Her surprise at discovering he had a sister was overshadowed by his insightful response.

She had not considered it before, but sometimes the house felt alive with memories of the past. She often imagined hearing her father's enthusiastic cries upon discovering a new Egyptian piece. Or seeing her mother's emotive expressions as she rehearsed her lines whilst looking in the mirror. The house was like a shrine to their memory, a reminder she was once part of a loving family, and she would never forsake them.

Tears threatened to fall.

"I want to be left alone," she whispered, looking down into her lap.

She wanted to be at home with her precious memories.

Mr. Stone placed his hand on the seat between them and edged a little closer to her. Suddenly, she wished she was alone with him in his carriage, wished to hear his salacious banter, wished he could ease the crippling feeling of loneliness that took hold of her in moments of weakness.

George shuffled to the edge of his chair and sat forward, his arms resting on his knees. "Perhaps I have gone about things in the wrong way," he confessed. "Is there nothing I can do or say to make you reconsider your place there?" When she shook her head, he gave a deep sigh. "Will you not at least agree to meet with me on occasion? It is what Father would have wanted."

Rebecca looked up at his angelic face. A stab of guilt hit her squarely in the chest. There was a softness to his features that reminded her so much of her father. Some part of her wanted to reach out to him, desperate for the comfort that comes with familiarity.

"You may call on me at the museum," she heard herself

say and was quick to add, "but no one else, only you and only on occasion."

"I should leave," Mr. Stone said, standing abruptly, and she could not determine whether his tone held a hint of sadness or hostility. "I shall leave you to talk privately. Will you arrange to see Miss Linwood home?"

George nodded. "Of course."

Mr. Stone seemed distant now, and she could feel him drifting further away from her, retreating to his private sanctuary and barring the door.

Her mind and body were fraught with anguish and pain: for the loss of her parents, for fear of being hurt by the Wellfords, for thinking Gabriel Stone would walk away and she would never see him again.

Knots formed in her stomach, and she wanted to jump up and beg him to stay, beg him not to leave her.

"Before you leave, Stone. Can you not persuade Rebecca to accompany me to Lord Chelton's ball this evening?"

There was an awkward moment of silence.

"I am not a gentleman who expresses excitement for such activities," he replied coldly. "Besides, Miss Linwood is capable of making up her own mind." He offered her a respectful bow and her fear turned to anger for his indifference.

"Yes, I will come with you tonight," she suddenly said, brandishing the words like a weapon with the intention of hurting Gabriel Stone.

He turned to face her, his stern countenance reminding her of the time she sat on his steps and watched him draw the curtains. The first time he'd shut her out. "Goodbye, Miss Linwood," he said, not "good day" or "good afternoon." "I trust you will have an enjoyable evening."

CHAPTER 10

*G*abriel strode from the house and jumped into his carriage, anger and disappointment escaping as a loud exasperated sigh.

The hard lump still pulsed in his throat, a lump that threatened to explode in a burst of uncontrollable fury at the sight of Lord Wellford playing the doting brother. He'd fought to suppress it, tried to swallow it down. Then Miss Linwood's firm stance faltered, and he felt her betrayal like strong hands around his neck, squeezing tightly until he could no longer breathe.

He'd not expected her to be fooled by her brother's soppy blue eyes and soft words. He'd assumed her sharp tongue would leave Wellford sore and bruised. And with steely determination, she would demand an apology. Yet like a naive debutante, she had fallen prey to his flowery charms.

Gabriel struggled to understand why he even cared.

Why could he not shake the feeling she had sided against him? Why was his mind so fraught with jealousy that all rational thought was lost to him?

Perhaps it had something to do with the fact Wellford

might prove to be the caring brother he could not be to his own sister—to the daughter of the woman who had taken his mother's place. There was no denying the irony of his situation. He could show Miss Linwood compassion but could not feel the same way about his own kin.

He threw his head back against the cushioned squab and inhaled deeply, only to find the sweet smell of lavender teasing his nostrils, drawing his thoughts back to the moment he first tasted Rebecca Linwood's lips.

Something had happened to him that night.

Her enchanting essence had penetrated his mind and body, igniting something deep inside that could not be extinguished.

In the past, he'd dabbled in the odd liaison, purely to sate a physical desire, purely to appease an appetite. Yet he had never felt a soul-deep connection before, never felt a blissful form of torture, an overwhelming need burning inside with such ferocious intensity.

Even now, as the muscles in his shoulders relaxed, and he welcomed the silence and solitude of his carriage, his vivid imagination refused to be tempered. Instead, he imagined her sitting astride him, moaning with pleasure as her hot body moulded around the length of him.

Good God!

What had happened to the man content to spend his days idling in his study with just a mound of old books for company?

By the time his carriage pulled into Hanover Square, he could feel the tension pounding behind his eyes, which was slightly less torturous than the pulsating of his heavy loins.

"Welcome home, sir," Cosgrove said in his usual lofty tone as his gaze lingered on Gabriel's furrowed brow. "I trust you've had an enjoyable afternoon."

79

If titles were given for sarcasm, his butler would be a duke.

"I believe my expression says it all," he replied, shrugging out of his coat.

"There is a package on your desk. I am certain it will improve your mood."

Gabriel walked into the study. He surveyed the cluttered desk like an eager father, expecting a rush of excitement when his children looked up and noticed he was home. However, the feeling of pleasant familiarity did not evolve into anything deeper.

In frustration, he strode over and picked up the package. Ripping off the paper, he hoped to rouse something more than a faint flicker of interest. He opened the top drawer, removed a pair of spectacles and put them on before scanning the leather cover for marks and flicking through the musty pages.

Terrasson's *The Life of Sethos* was a fictional work examining the private memoirs of the ancient Egyptians. With a glass of brandy in one hand and his book in the other, Gabriel moved to the sofa. It would take him hours to read through Terrasson's work. With his mind preoccupied, he would forget all about Rebecca Linwood delighting the guests at Lord Chelton's ball with her dazzling smile and generous bosom.

Gabriel read eight pages of the preface before his lids grew heavy and he became conscious of the fact he was struggling to stay awake. Eight pages became ten and then twelve and then—nothing.

Somewhere in a dark recess of his mind, he heard the faint strains of a waltz. The triple beat called to him, forced him to concentrate, forced him to focus his gaze. At first, he imagined himself outside. A hazy mist floated up to obscure his view, only clearing when he willed it to do so.

He saw her then, his bewitching temptress. She shone like a bright star in a black sky, illuminating the ballroom with all the power of a hundred-candle chandelier.

Pushing away from the doorjamb, he tried to take a step forward. But the chain around his ankle pulled him back, tearing into his flesh as a reminder of his folly.

"Let me go," he cried. But he could only stand and stare as some other gentleman kissed her hand, as some other gentleman danced with her and pressed too close to her luscious body. "Rebecca," he yelled, punching the air with clenched fists.

But she could not hear him.

"Wake up, sir."

Cosgrove's voice penetrated his addled brain, and he opened his eyes, blinking a few times and shaking his head until his butler had two eyes and not four.

"Thank goodness," Cosgrove said. "I thought you'd been taken by a fever."

Gabriel sat up, removed his spectacles and glanced around the room. "What time is it?" he asked, noticing the solitary candle on the side table.

"It is almost nine. I know how you hate to be disturbed when you're reading, but I heard shouting."

"Thank you, Cosgrove." He scanned the sofa for his book and located it on the floor next to the glass of brandy. "I must have fallen asleep."

"Shall I ask Mrs. Hudson to prepare supper, sir?"

Gabriel sat forward, his elbows resting on his knees, and let his head fall into his hands. "Yes. Just a light repast will suffice," he muttered, wondering why he still felt so detached from reality.

The dream had been vivid. So much so, he knew if he closed his eyes he would still be there, still watching other men fawn over his prize. With a deep sigh, he picked up the book and flicked to the first chapter. Usually, his hunger for knowledge would have him devouring every page. Now, another passion occupied his thoughts: an eagerness to discover everything there was to know about Rebecca Linwood. An intense craving to educate himself in the needs of her body consumed him, too.

Without another thought, he jumped up and made for the door. "Cosgrove," he shouted, the word echoing through the oak-lined hallway.

The butler stopped at the end of the corridor and ambled back towards him as though he had missed the urgency in his master's voice. "You called, sir?"

"Have the tray sent up to my room. I shall eat while I dress."

Cosgrove glanced dubiously at his master's attire. "Dress, sir?"

"Yes, Cosgrove," Gabriel replied, taking the stairs two at a time. "I am going out."

"Where on earth have you been hiding this beauty?" Mr. Ingram said, lifting his monocle to his left eye and squinting with his right.

Rebecca flinched, as though ice-cold fingers were creeping slowly up her spine. Mr. Ingram was not the first gentleman to compliment her this evening. He was not the first gentleman to ogle her like a prized bit of beef. Thankfully, the man's portly stomach prevented him from stepping any closer.

"My sister has been rusticating in the country," Lord

Wellford blurted, no doubt fearing she would tell another man she actually worked for a living.

Mr. Ingram's gaze followed the line of her throat, down to the plunging neckline of her mother's only white gown. He moved the eyeglass back and forth to determine the best view.

Rebecca thought to inform him that market day was on Thursday, but George coughed into his fist to wake the gentleman from his musings.

"I trust you have a place left on your dance card for me?" Ingram asked.

Rebecca shook her head. Even if she'd wanted to be friendly, she refused to dance with a man who wore rouge.

"I'm afraid not." She ignored George's frustrated sigh.

George put his hand on her elbow and turned her away from a disappointed Mr. Ingram. "You must dance with someone," he whispered.

Her father was the only gentleman she had ever danced with. As soon as she'd turned sixteen, he insisted on hiring a dance tutor. But feeling awkward and clumsy, Rebecca had begged and pleaded with him to tutor her himself. She loved those moments alone with him. She loved the attention, loved his devotion and often feigned ignorance in learning the steps in the hope of extending the lesson.

When Mr. Ingram finally departed, Rebecca felt the rush of relief quickly turn to anger. "I did not agree to accompany you so you could parade me about like a debutante desperate for a place on the marriage mart."

In truth, she did not really know why she'd agreed to accompany him. The words had just tumbled out of her mouth. Her thoughts had been jumbled, plagued with guilt, her nerves teetering on a precipice. And George reminded her so much of her father. When she'd sensed Gabriel Stone step behind his wall of indifference, she felt an overwhelming urge to prove that her life was perfectly fine without him in it.

"Rebecca, you need to start living in the real world, instead of being stuck in some stuffy room surrounded by objects belonging to the dead."

It was rather sad George felt that way. Perhaps there was no room for passion in his life; perhaps the chains of duty and responsibility hung too heavily around his neck. The Egyptian museum was as much a part of her as her heart or her lungs. Nothing would ever change that.

"I am beginning to distrust your motives for asking me here," she said, deciding his burden of duty included seeing her wed. "Mr. Ingram is the fifth unmarried gentleman you have introduced me to this evening. Does living in the real world not extend to meeting other young ladies, too?"

George sneered. "Your future is all that is important to me, Rebecca. Despite being beautiful you have no fortune, and there are some men who will shy away from the circumstance of your birth. Marriage is not a curse. It is an aspiration shared by all ladies living in the real world."

What a fool she was. George was only concerned with marrying her off. Her brother professed to have her interests at heart, yet he managed to say and do the wrong thing at every turn. Indeed, she had made another mistake in trusting him.

"My museum is the real world to me," she said, determined to make it clear she wasn't some pawn to be sacrificed for the greater good. "This ... this place is just a cesspit of iniquity. Perhaps I should pin a tag to my gown that says 'one hundred and fifty guineas, but beware of minor defaults.'"

George waved his hand in the air. "You're being ridiculous. All I want is for you to be happy."

"Happy?" she mocked. "Can you not hear the hypocrisy

in your own words? You wish me to marry a man I do not love, so long as he can provide material comforts and over-look the nature of my birth. To you, that is an admirable choice: to sell one's soul for wealth and respectability. Well, I would rather join the urchins scouring the streets, begging for scraps."

"You cannot condemn me for trying to legitimise your position."

Rebecca sucked in a breath.

There was no reasoning with this man. "I am suddenly relieved I am illegitimate. The irony of legitimacy is that it appears to be defined by a lack of morals and a severe lack of integrity."

Without another word, she pushed past him and stormed out through the open doors onto the terrace. She paced back and forth until her breathing slowed to its usual rate.

Thankfully, George chose not to follow and so she took a moment to look out over the garden, placing the palms of her hands on the stone wall and relishing the feel of the cool breeze.

She should never have agreed to come.

Her thoughts drifted back to earlier in the day, to the way Gabriel Stone had devoured her with his sinful eyes, to the way her body responded so eagerly to him. Tonight, numerous gentlemen had looked at her in a similar way. Yet it felt different, unnatural.

It felt wrong.

Gabriel affected her like no one else before. He had found a way into her heart. Even though she was alone on the terrace, it felt as though a part of him was still with her.

Was it possible to develop deep feelings after just a few short days?

The thought that he would not be lounging on her chaise

when she returned home caused a pain in her throat, making it feel uncomfortable to breathe. She closed her eyes and tried to conjure an image of him.

"Ah, there you are, Miss Wellford."

A deep, husky tone penetrated her reverie. The image of Gabriel's mischievous grin dissolved into nothing as she opened her eyes.

Rebecca swung around to face the gentleman who, with his black hair and hawk-like eyes, had all the appeal of Satan.

"My name is Miss Linwood," she said haughtily.

"Then please accept my apology, Miss Linwood." He stepped forward in the slippery way men do when their words are not in accordance with their lecherous intentions. "I saw you were alone and thought you might like to dance."

He moved closer and took her gloved hand, brought it to his lips and held it there for longer than deemed appropriate.

"I'm afraid I do not dance." She pulled her hand free, struggled to keep her tone even, for his eyes appeared cold and detached, despite his friendly protestations. "And my brother is waiting for me."

As she stepped aside to walk around him, he moved to block her exit. "Your brother is otherwise occupied. I, on the other hand, am not." His beady, black eyes fell to her lips before dropping to the exposed curve of her bosom.

"As I have already told you," she said, swallowing away her fear, "I do not dance."

"Good. It was not really dancing I had in mind."

Rebecca lifted her chin. "It is not prudent to be so forward with a lady, sir."

He gave a devilish grin. "Now, Miss Linwood, can you really call yourself a lady? In my experience, those with questionable lineage tend to have questionable morals."

This man was a scoundrel, a rogue. Suddenly, the

crowded ballroom seemed much more the better option.

When Rebecca tried to move past him, he grabbed her arm. "Come now, there is nothing to fear. I suggest we go out into the garden and find something to titillate our fancy."

"What I suggest is that you remove your hand from the lady's arm," Gabriel Stone growled, his threatening tone slicing through the air. "Unless you're happy to choke on your own teeth."

Rebecca's desperate gaze met Gabriel's, and she drank in the glorious sight of him, let the warm feeling flood her body, banishing all her doubts and fears.

The gentleman turned around to face him. But on surveying the breadth of Gabriel's chest loosened his grip to let Rebecca pull her arm free.

Gabriel held out his hand to her, and she wanted to run into his strong embrace, wanted to fling her arms around his neck and lay her head upon his chest. Instead, she drifted towards him. When he took her hand and placed it in the crook of his arm, the intoxicating feel of his hard body next to hers caused a momentary stumble.

"Come, let me escort you home," he said, supporting her as they walked back into the ballroom. "It is that or I will murder the man."

The first few strains of a waltz drifted through the air. The sound roused memories of her father's excitement on his return home from Vienna, eager to show them the dance popular all over Europe. Indeed, she could still hear him humming in tune as he took her in his arms and they glided about the room. She missed him terribly. The ache in her heart had never really healed.

But there was only one man who could ease her pain now.

She gripped his arm a little tighter, looked up into those welcoming eyes. "Dance with me, Gabriel," she whispered.

CHAPTER 11

*G*abriel looked down into the most enthralling pair of emerald eyes he had ever seen and found, despite all his reservations, he could not refuse her request.

"You do dance?" Her gaze drifted over his face as she waited for his reply.

"I do, but often under duress and on very rare occasions."

Rebecca smiled. "I have only ever danced with my father." Her eyes brightened as though recalling a happy memory. "But I would like to dance with you, Gabriel."

Her words caused a strange sensation in the pit of his stomach; the feeling flooded his body, relaxing his rigid shoulders. He forgot he wanted to throttle the dissolute rogue and kick him across the garden until his fancy truly was titillated.

"Then it will be my pleasure to dance with you, Miss Linwood."

"Rebecca," she whispered. The corners of her mouth curled up into another sweet smile. "Call me Rebecca."

He had no time to think, no time to prepare for how it

would feel to hold her in his arms. The music was in full stride, the floor littered with circling couples. With a firm grip, he drew her closer, felt a jolt of desire shoot through his body as he took her hand in his and led her out onto the floor.

That first dance, his for longer than he could remember, should have been awkward, their movements lumbered and untutored given their lack of experience. Yet their bodies were in perfect tune, gliding effortlessly about the floor. Indeed, he forgot he was in a crowded ballroom. His only thoughts were of her.

Rebecca looked up at him. Her soft bosom heaved with excitement. Her moist lips parted, as her eyes glazed with a look of euphoria. Heaven help him. He could think of nothing other than her naked body writhing beneath him as she moaned his name in the wild throes of passion. His eager manhood stirred in response, and he knew that if he were to survive the next few minutes, he would have to distract his mind.

"You look beautiful tonight," he said in the hope conversation would ease his predicament, but his choice of words did nothing to dampen his desire. "You should not have gone out onto the terrace alone," he was quick to add.

He'd seen her from the other side of the ballroom, seen the rakish gentleman stalk after her like a wildcat on the prowl and the memory helped to cool his heated blood.

"I should not have agreed to come," she said honestly. "Regardless of what George believes, I do not belong here with these people."

No, she was far too good for them.

"Neither do I," he said, and he could still hear the low hum of desire evident in his voice. "I have always felt more comfortable with my books."

Rebecca smiled. "I had it on good authority you were a recluse," she said as her dress swished around his legs just to tease him. "Now, here you are at your second ball in a matter of a few days."

The question "Why did you come?" was buried implicitly within her words.

He could have said it had always been his intention to attend. Lord Chelton had been a friend of his father's. But he found he could not lie to her. This madness that had taken hold of him seemed determined to drag him through an emotional version of hell.

"I came here because I wanted to see you." Instead of feeling awkward, it felt quite liberating to convey some sense of what plagued his thoughts. Even so, he chose not to add that jealousy had played its part, too. "I should not have left you alone with Lord Wellford. Despite the fact he's your brother, I do not trust his intentions."

There was an odd look on her face, one of pleasure mixed with intrigue. "You are right. He seems determined to see me wed and has introduced me to a whole host of bizarre characters." She gave a sweet sigh. "He looks so much like my father I forget I hardly know him. Perhaps now you understand why it suits me to think of him as my father's son."

"Well, your father's son is standing on the edge of the ballroom watching us dance. His glare of disapproval is unmistakable."

Gabriel noticed her examine the crowd as he twirled her around the floor. "Oh, he is just grumpy because I refused to dance with all the gentlemen he introduced me to. I stated quite categorically that I do not dance."

Gabriel slid his hand further along her back. He firmed his grip before swinging her around a little too quickly, forcing her to suck in a deep breath. When her fingers gripped his shoulder, and her vibrant gaze met his, she laughed.

"Then let us show him the reason why you chose to dance with me," he said, aware of the hint of possessiveness in his tone.

"It was me who asked you to dance, remember," she said with some amusement.

"Yes, but I have wanted to ask you from the moment I met you and so you must have read my thoughts." If only she could truly read his thoughts, as he would like her to ask him to do something far more lascivious.

Rebecca did not answer him, but the flicker of desire in her eyes told him all he needed to know. He did not take his eyes off hers for what remained of the dance. Locked together, they moved about the room, forgetting everyone and everything.

He felt her gaze like a lover's caress, calming and soothing, penetrating his soul, and he matched it with the same level of intensity. When a mischievous grin threatened to play at the corners of her mouth, he felt the flames within burn brighter and he wondered if he would ever sate this overwhelming need for her.

When the music stopped, a sense of disappointment fell over him. And as he escorted her from the floor, he struggled to shake it.

"Thank you for dancing with me. I know how much it must have pained you."

The only pain he felt was an ache in his groin. "It was my pleasure."

"Would you mind escorting me home?" she whispered, the words meant for his ears alone. "I do not want to ask George as he will taunt me with my father's smile, and for some strange reason, I do not feel strong enough to fight it tonight."

"Of course," he said, inclining his head. He understood what she meant. He did not have the strength to fight this attraction anymore. "But we will need to tell Lord Wellford you intend to leave."

She nodded solemnly. "Very well."

They did not need to seek Lord Wellford out, as he moved towards them as soon as they left the dance floor. "I would like a word with you, Rebecca. That is if you can drag yourself away from your friend Mr. Stone."

There was no mistaking the vehemence in his voice.

"Miss Linwood and I are leaving," Gabriel said, deciding to offer no further explanation. Wellford could not offer a rebuke or deem their decision inappropriate. Rebecca had been without the protection of her father for a few years. In his opinion, Wellford had left it too late to attempt to step into the role.

"Then go fetch your cape, Rebecca. I shall keep Mr. Stone company until you return."

She looked up at Gabriel, uncertainty clouding her eyes, and so he nodded towards the hall.

As she walked away, Lord Wellford led him to a quieter corner of the room. "I do not know what understanding exists between the two of you," he snarled, "but I doubt it is simply a case of friends and business associates."

"And what leads you to that conclusion? Is it the fact the lady danced with someone of her own choosing?"

Wellford looked over his shoulder. "You may fool yourself, Stone, but I doubt there is a person in this room who doesn't know how much you want her. I'm sure the prospect of owning an Egyptian museum is a rather attractive incentive."

Gabriel thought of grabbing the lord by his fancy cravat

and throttling him. "Perhaps I should provide you with an extensive list of my assets. Perhaps then you would know I have no need to make decisions based on financial gain. My only motivation is her safety and to offer my protection."

"As her brother, it is my responsibility to offer her protection."

"Protection?" Gabriel sneered. "Where were you when I saved her from being ravished in the garden? Where were you when she was scared out of her wits? Oh, that's right. You were the one responsible for letting her believe she was cursed." Gabriel took a step closer, his height giving him the advantage to look down on Wellford. "I don't care who you are," he said through gritted teeth. "If you hurt her again, you will answer to me."

Gabriel stepped back and scanned the gentleman from head to toe. "Good evening, Lord Wellford," he said, turning on his heels.

"You're no good for her, Stone," Wellford mumbled behind him. "You're even more obsessed with the dead than she is."

Gabriel ordered his coachman, Higson, to take Miss Linwood home and gave the impression he should return for him later. Although certain allowances could be made due to Rebecca's circumstances, Gabriel did not want to draw undue attention to her or be the topic of conversation in the best salons. So after stepping inside to have a brief conversation with his host, he slipped back out and made his way to the bottom of Berkeley Street before turning the corner to find Higson waiting in Manchester Square.

"You could have warned me you were not coming with me," Rebecca said as he settled back into the seat opposite. She pulled her cloak tighter across her chest, and he read it as her way of punishing him.

"I am coming with you," he said, after taking a moment to catch his breath. "I was just a few minutes behind."

They sat in silence for a while, and he was aware of her gaze searching his face before falling to his mouth.

"What did George have to say?" she eventually said. "He did not look very pleased."

"He believes my interests in you run deeper than that of a business partner or friend. He thinks my morbid fascination with the dead is not good for you."

She shot forward, her cloak falling away, presenting him with luscious mounds of creamy-white flesh. "That's absurd. There is nothing morbid about your interest in the ancient world. You are a scholar. I am the one who collects objects belonging to the dead."

Gabriel winced. That was not entirely true. Thankfully, she had not seen the laboratory in his cellar.

"You have not said anything about my first comment. About the fact he believes my interest in you to be disreputable."

She raised an arched brow and her lips curved into a flirtatious smile. "What is there to say? I am fully aware of your immoral intentions, Gabriel. But I wonder if you are aware of mine."

Desire hit him like a lightning bolt, surging through his body at a remarkable rate. It was so strong he bounced off the seat. Then he noticed his carriage had stopped abruptly, and he looked out of the window to see the elegant facade of Miss Linwood's museum.

Hell and damnation.

"I shall help you out." Gabriel threw open the door and jumped down to the pavement. The cool night air brought instant relief from the liquid fire flowing through his veins. He offered his assistance, his hand gripping her fingers for longer than was necessary. "And I shall see you safely inside."

As they neared the front door, she glanced up at him coyly, suggesting her thoughts mirrored his own. "You are welcome to come in," she said, struggling to hold his gaze.

He had never received a more tempting invitation. It would take a pack of wolves gnawing at his ankles to keep him out. But as he opened his mouth to speak, her house-keeper opened the door to greet them.

"Mrs. James," Rebecca said with some surprise. "What are you doing here at this late hour?"

Mrs. James' suspicious gaze moved back and forth between them as she sucked in her cheeks. "Mr. Pearce told me about this dreadful business with the curse. I thought I would wait until you came home. I thought it might bring some peace of mind to know the house was secure." She glanced at Gabriel in a way that made him want to drop to his knees, confess all of his sins and beg for forgiveness. "I thought it might help if you knew you were not alone, that there was someone here to check in on you before you retired for the evening."

Disappointment sizzled in his ears. The woman had as good as trampled all over his flaming desire.

"That's very kind of you, Mrs. James." Rebecca looked up at him. "Isn't that kind, Mr. Stone?"

"Very kind," he repeated, wondering if George Wellford was the pack leader of this particular wolf.

"Mr. Stone was kind enough to escort me home."

Judging by the look on her housekeeper's face, she may as well have said he had escorted her home with the intention of tearing her clothes from her body and ravishing her in the doorway.

Mrs. James followed the conversation and then offered to take Miss Linwood's cape.

"Well, I should go." He hovered at the door, his good mood well and truly ruined. A feeling mirrored by Miss Linwood's strained smile. "Good night, Miss Linwood."

"Good night, Mr. Stone," she whispered as she walked inside and closed the door.

CHAPTER 12

his was not how Rebecca imagined the night would end.

Instead of warm masculine fingers trailing a seductive line over the buttons of her gown, Mrs. James' chubby stumps were pulling and yanking at the delicate objects with all the grace of a chimpanzee.

"There, I've done it," she said with a gasp, helping Rebecca to step out of it before draping it over the chair.

Once in her nightdress, she sat on the stool in front of the dressing table to remove the pins from her hair. Again, she imagined Gabriel's deft fingers caressing the copper locks.

From the moment he rescued her on the terrace, to the moment she said good night on the doorstep, she was preoccupied with an overwhelming need to sate an inner craving for him. A craving so potent she could not define it in words.

"I … I hear Mr. Stone has agreed to become a partner in the museum," Mrs. James said as she helped Rebecca take down her coiffure.

"I'm sorry I didn't mention it before, but we've only just agreed on the details."

Rebecca had no idea why the lie fell so easily from her lips. It was not as though they were trying to discover the identity of the intruder and needed a cover story. There was no reason for Gabriel Stone to spend any more time at the museum.

"I'm sure Mr. Stone is a respectable gentleman. I know it's not my place to say anything, it's just sometimes a man can mistake a friendly countenance for something else, for something more …"

Rebecca was touched by her housekeeper's words, even though she hoped Mr. Stone *had* misread her friendly countenance for something far more sinful.

"Thank you for your concern, Mrs. James, but there is no need to worry."

That was another lie. There was every need to worry. Rebecca could not stop her heart from beating rapidly in his presence. She could not stop desire unfurling in her stomach at the sound of his voice. She could not stop her body from burning at the slightest touch of his fingers.

"I'm sure you're right," Mrs. James said with a nod. "Well, now you're all settled I'd best be on my way."

"It must be nearly midnight," Rebecca replied, trying to distract her mind from thoughts of Gabriel Stone. "Surely you're not walking home?"

Mrs. James smiled as she opened the door. "No. Our eldest, Tom, came to meet me. He's been in the kitchen for the last hour, tucking into a bowl of broth. No need to follow me down," she said. "Mr. Pearce gave me his key, so I'll lock the door on my way out."

A tinge of guilt pricked Rebecca's conscience for feeling so annoyed at the housekeeper's untimely presence. And she did feel a sense of relief knowing Mr. Pearce could not enter the building without her knowledge.

"Thank you for waiting, Mrs. James. I shall see you in the morning."

As Rebecca brushed out her hair, she listened to the housekeeper's heavy gait plodding down the stairs. Being on the third floor, she heard nothing else after that.

Life was so much simpler when she had no one to think of but herself. Being alone had many advantages. There was no pressing need to forge alliances with estranged family. No feelings of guilt hanging around one's neck like thick links of chain—no feelings of disappointment.

As she climbed into bed, her thoughts drifted back to Gabriel. Being alone also meant no more passionate kisses, no more flirtatious banter to thaw her frozen heart. No heated glances or dreams of love.

Thoughts of love and loneliness drove sleep away from her door. As an hour passed, she did everything she could to clear her muddled mind: closed her eyes and listened to the rain hammer against the windowpane, took long deep breaths to calm her restless body.

In the end she got up, decided to make a pot of tea and read a few pages of her father's notebook.

The floor felt cold beneath her feet. The breeze blowing in from behind the shutters caused her to shiver, and so she shuffled back into her dancing slippers and grabbed the silk cloak off the chair.

Even in an empty house, there was something about the dark that made one conscious of making the slightest sound. But as she padded quietly across the landing to the top of the stairs, the faint hum of silence was not the only thing she heard. This time, the whispering wasn't coming from the storeroom, but from inside the Egyptian museum and she tried to think of a rational explanation to calm her racing heart.

Perhaps Tom hadn't finished eating his broth. Perhaps Mrs. James had decided to potter about while waiting. Rebecca thought to call out to her, but the distinctively masculine voices broke the silence.

"I have not come here to look at a pile of dusty old stones."

"Shush. Be quiet, or you'll wake her up."

"That is my intention."

Rebecca gripped the handrail, fear creeping through her veins like a vine, wrapping itself around her throat until she could hardly breathe. She could hear two voices, their eloquent tone suggesting they were not thieves from the rookery, but privileged men of the aristocracy.

"Give me that. You've drunk far more than your share."

"Perhaps we should locate her room and introduce ourselves."

"I told you. There is something I need to do here."

"I can wait. I suppose the thrill of anticipation heats the blood."

Every muscle in her body grew taut, and she struggled to swallow.

She had to get out of the house. Yet the overwhelming need to protect her father's relics caused an internal war to rage. Images of shattered vases and smashed stone tablets flooded her mind. Perhaps she should confront these men, hoping they were true gentlemen beneath all the bravado and simply up to drunken mischief?

Then she heard her father's voice in her head telling her to run. Without another thought, she forced her hesitant feet to move quickly down the stairs, before slipping out into the street in the dead of night.

The rain fell hard, lashing off the stone paving, soaking through her dainty slippers in just a few short strides.

Blinking away the rivulets trickling down her face, she hurried along Piccadilly. Her legs knew the route she wanted to take even though her mind was unable to string together any coherent thoughts.

By the time she reached New Bond Street, she was out of breath. But she continued running, despite the searing pain in her chest and the burning in her throat. The faster she ran, the heavier her garments became, the sodden material sticking to her body like a second skin.

When she finally reached Hanover Square, she threw herself at Gabriel's door and pounded it with numb fists.

The sombre clip of shoes on the tiled floor beyond alerted her of the butler's approach. When he eventually opened the door and peered out, the gap was barely wide enough to fit a boot. His disapproving gaze scanned her from head to toe, and she knew he would not let her inside.

With all the strength she could muster, she barged past him. "Gabriel!" she cried, running into all the rooms off the hall. "Gabriel."

The butler tried to grab her arm, but she shrank out of his hold and ran up the stairs, banging on every closed door. "Gabriel."

Eventually, a door opened at the end of the landing and Gabriel hurried out. His breeches hung loosely from his waist as he threw a shirt over his head.

"Rebecca," he said with some surprise. "What's wrong? What's happened?" He turned to face the irate butler, whose ragged breathing sounded more like hoarse grunts. "All is well, Cosgrove. I am acquainted with Miss Linwood. You may go back to bed."

The butler's horrified gaze fell to the puddle of water at her feet.

"It's the museum," she panted, wishing she could run into

Gabriel's arms, wishing he could soothe away all her troubles. "There are men ... there are men in the museum."

Gabriel rushed over and took her hands in his. "My God, your hands are cold and your lips are blue."

"I ran ... I ran all the way here."

Gabriel's brow furrowed. "You're wet through. Cosgrove, find some towels and wake Mrs. Hudson. Miss Linwood will need a bath and some dry clothes."

Rebecca gripped Gabriel's forearm, the hard muscle flexing beneath her touch. "If they damage anything," she said, holding back the tears. "I cannot lose my father's relics."

Gabriel raised his hand and brushed the wet tendrils of hair from her face, his fingers tracing the line of her jaw. "How many men were there?"

"Two. I think there were two."

"Come, you can sit in my room. The fire is still burning in the grate. You may take your bath in there." He swung back around to his butler. "Wake Higson and tell him to have the horses ready in five minutes. He is to accompany me to Miss Linwood's house."

Cosgrove glanced at his master, and Rebecca could have sworn the beginnings of a smile threatened to play on his grim lips. "Very well, sir," he said, before trudging back down the stairs.

Gabriel led her into his room. The intimacy of the gesture caused her desperate need for him to resurface. He led her over to the fire and removed the wet cloak from her shoulders, letting it fall to the floor.

"Come and sit," he said, pulling the chair closer to the fire before guiding her to the seat. "I must get dressed, but we will talk when I return."

Rebecca nodded and turned her attention to the fiery

flickers, rubbing her hands together in front of them in a bid to stop her from turning around.

"Do you think they will still be there?" she said, scanning what she could see of the forest-green walls and dark furniture. The room had an inherently masculine feel, a heavy brooding intensity that reflected the character of its owner to perfection. The potent smell of wood and spice brought back memories of their illicit kiss.

"I hope so," he growled, and she glanced over her shoulder to see him pulling on his boots. He came to stand at her side, and she felt a large reassuring hand on her shoulder. "Mrs. Hudson will provide anything you need. I shall be back shortly."

She looked up into sinful brown eyes. "If they have damaged anything. If they have—"

When he placed his finger on her lips, she felt a tremor shake her body and had a sudden urge to kiss it, to feel it trace the outline of her mouth. "Do not talk of it until we know for sure."

Gabriel planted a chaste kiss on her forehead and hurried from the room with purposeful strides. It suddenly occurred to her that since her father's death she had been living a lie.

Despite her independence, despite her ability to provide for herself, she was weak and useless without the protection of a man. The thought roused memories of lonely suppers, of having no one to talk to about her hopes and dreams, of lying cold and unloved in her bed.

Thankfully, Rebecca's melancholic mood was broken by the sound of the door opening and a tall, slim woman entered. Her tired eyes caused her features to look even more severe than her hollow cheeks suggested. "I'm Mrs. Hudson, the housekeeper," she said, her soft voice contradicting her countenance. "Let's get you behind the screen and out of those wet clothes. Cosgrove will stoke the fire while the footman fills the tub."

The intimate space suddenly thrummed with activity as the staff busied about, coming to the aid of a stranger.

Although Rebecca noticed the curious glances darting between them, no one asked any questions or gave the impression there was anything untoward in a young lady turning up half dressed in the middle of the night. Indeed, they almost looked pleased at the prospect.

When it came to getting into the tub, her toes were so cold the water pained her. It took three attempts until they grew accustomed to the temperature. Rebecca bent her knees so she could rest her head on the back of the copper bath. The warm water lapped over her aching bones, and she cupped it in her hands and swished it over her shoulders.

This was where he bathed, she thought, knowing this obsession she had for him was like a living thing growing inside of her. She could almost feel him in the room. His exotic smell fed her addiction, and she closed her eyes and let the essence of the man she had grown so attached to calm her restless soul.

CHAPTER 13

*G*abriel rode through the rain as though Lucifer was chasing his tail. Higson said nothing about being woken from his bed or about the nature of their business. But Gabriel saw him slip his homemade cudgel into his coat pocket. The lead-filled goat's horn was heavy enough to render a man unconscious.

After tethering the horses to the railings outside Rebecca's house, Gabriel tried the front door to find it open.

"We'll move through the house together," he whispered, casting a dubious eye over Higson's stocky frame as the man equipped his weapon. "Try to be quiet."

Once inside, Gabriel listened out for the sound of voices, for footsteps and creaking floorboards, but heard nothing. And so, by way of numerous hand gestures, he conveyed the order in which they would check the downstairs rooms.

With regimental precision, they moved through the house and once they had established it was empty, Gabriel sent Higson to search the lower floors for signs of theft or damage while he examined the third floor.

He knew why he had chosen to check that particular floor, why he found himself drawn down the dark corridor to Rebecca's bedchamber. After all, she was currently lying naked in his bathtub, and the thought had him in a state of semi-arousal.

As he ran his fingers over her counterpane and trailed them down the hangings on her bed, he wondered if she was doing a similar thing. The image of her eager hands running over his private things caused another surge of excitement. Indeed, the need to hurry home forced him to expedite his task with more speed and efficiency.

He found no physical signs of disturbance, not until he reached the parlour, and the sight forced him to stand and stare in frozen silence.

The painting of Rebecca's mother stood upright on the chair opposite the door. However, the gilt edges now framed a canvas of diagonal slashes slicing right through the image, severing the angelic face.

Gabriel's heart sank to the pit of his stomach. The vision of Rebecca's tortured expression haunted his thoughts. He imagined her dropping to her knees while he struggled to find the right words of comfort.

"There's no damage downstairs," Higson said, trudging into the room, taking care not to step on the rug with his dirty boots. "But someone's forced the door leading to the basement." He came to stand at Gabriel's side and jerked his head towards the painting. "Looks like whatever's happened here is personal."

It was an insightful comment. Higson had no idea the portrait was of Rebecca's mother. The coachman's assessment was based on the way the culprit had displayed his work. Gabriel's immediate thought was to blame George

Wellford, but then he dismissed the idea. Although George's methods were underhanded and thoughtless, he would never intentionally hurt Rebecca, not like this.

"Do not speak a word of this to anyone, not until I have told Miss Linwood."

"Is it valuable?"

"Its value is purely sentimental," Gabriel said as he drew his hand down his face and sighed.

"Then I can't say as I envy you the task."

Gabriel cursed. "What the hell am I supposed to say?"

"I've always found the truth works well enough."

"Even when you know the truth will hurt?"

Higson shrugged. "Aye, even then."

Gabriel strode over, picked up the painting and put it behind the chair, out of view. "I don't want her to see it displayed like a blasted trophy," he said, feeling the need to explain his actions. He turned back to Higson. "Is the basement door secure?"

Higson scratched his head. "For the time being. But you'll need to get someone to look at it tomorrow."

Gabriel nodded. "I'll check the museum again before we leave, but it may be too difficult to make a proper assessment of the antiquities until daylight."

They wandered around the Egyptian displays, peering into the cabinets, searching for anything untoward.

"There should be four stone tablets on the plinth," Gabriel said, shouting commands through the darkness.

"They're all here, but I noticed an empty plinth in the hallway."

Gabriel recalled Rebecca mentioning an accident, a bust falling onto the stairs. "I know. There was some sort of incident with a bust of Nefertiti. Everything else seems to be in order," he said, though wondered why the culprit had targeted that specific painting. "We should head back."

During the ride back to Hanover Square, Gabriel's mind was plagued by uncertainty and doubt. His head urged him to go back and remove the damaged portrait, to tell Rebecca it had been stolen. His heart reminded him he was not capable of such deceit.

Of course, he also had another problem—Rebecca Linwood would be sleeping in his house.

The thought caused his heart to pound against his ribs. He could not deny that he wanted her with every ounce of his being. He ached at the thought of feeling her warm body curled up next to him in bed. Knowing temptation would be just a few short feet away was more than his weak body could bear. Yet he could not ask her to go to Lord Wellford's house, not in the middle of the night, and he could not expect her to return home.

In all the years of studying the dead, he had never encountered such complications. His work always brought him a level of peace and comfort. A feeling he craved. Now, his craving was in the form of a luscious flame-haired beauty. Now, immoral images played havoc with his thoughts, every action controlled by his rampant desire.

This delicious form of torture had given him a renewed optimism for life. And Rebecca had given every indication she was just as eager for his companionship.

What harm would it do to ease their physical torment?

As an independent woman of means, she had never alluded to love or marriage, which in itself was a blessing. He was not capable of loving anyone, not anymore. That didn't stop them exploring the realm of carnal pleasures. Perhaps it was time to be a little more spontaneous, to take Rebecca Linwood to his bed and to hell with the consequences.

Cosgrove's veiled sarcasm hit him as soon as he came through the door. "Your guest is washed and watered and resting in her room, sir," he said, helping Gabriel out of his wet coat. "If that is all, I shall retire for the rest of the evening."

Gabriel raised a curious brow. "In her room?" he repeated, the sense of disappointment that she was not waiting for him in his private chamber created a hollow feeling in his chest.

"You're back." Miss Linwood's tone conveyed her impatience, and as she rushed down the stairs to greet him, his gaze fell to her bare feet.

If he had to make a list of the attributes he found desirable in a woman, feet would not be amongst them. Yet he found the sight of her pretty toes oddly arousing.

As she came to stand in front of him, wearing nothing more than a nightdress and wrapper, her wide eyes searched his face. "Did you find them? Were they still there?"

Gabriel shook his head. "No. They'd left before we arrived."

Cosgrove gave a discreet cough and excused himself.

"What about the antiquities?" She paused and swallowed deeply. "Tell me everything is all right. Please tell me nothing is broken."

"As far as I could tell, everything in the museum is exactly as it should be." He would wait until morning to tell her about the painting as he suspected she would charge over there to assess the damage.

She placed her hand over her heart and closed her eyes briefly as she tried to regulate her breathing. "You don't know how relieved I am to hear you say that. While I was in the bathtub, I imagined you telling me they had destroyed my father's things and I … I don't think I could bear it."

His stomach churned at the thought of her seeing the tattered image of her mother.

"Perhaps we should call Lord Wellford. You could stay with him for a few days while we try to establish what is going on." The words sounded solemn. It was the last thing he wanted to do, but he knew it was the appropriate thing to say.

A look of panic flashed across her face. "I can't. Please, you mustn't tell him, Gabriel. Can I not stay here, just for tonight, just until I decide what to do?"

"Rebecca, people will talk. While I can guarantee the silence of my staff, I cannot be held accountable for the actions of meddling gossips."

She stepped closer and placed a hesitant palm on his chest. "Please, Gabriel. You're the only person I can trust."

He could not decide if it was the touching words or the warmth radiating from her hand that caused his heated blood to bubble with pleasure. "The choice is yours," he conceded easily. "I will do whatever makes you happy, Rebecca."

Even in the muted light, she glowed with a radiance he found irresistible, and he knew he would struggle to say no to her.

"Thank you." The words were barely a whisper as her hand fell from his chest. "I should go to bed."

She stood on her toes and pressed her lips to his cheek. He closed his eyes and inhaled the unique scent of her skin, let her brightness penetrate the layers of his clothing until his body tingled in response.

When she turned away from him, he could not find the words to convey the emotion that filled his chest. "Good night, Rebecca," he whispered as the muscles in his stomach twisted into painful knots of despair.

Despite finding the courage to give Gabriel a chaste kiss, he did not call after her. Rebecca walked up the stairs as though weights were strapped to her ankles, making each step harder to take.

What had she thought would happen? That he would wrap his strong arms around her and pull her into a passionate embrace?

She had felt his body tremble at the touch of her lips, felt the war raging inside him; an inner turmoil she suspected was more than a match for her own. He was hiding something of himself, perhaps the reason he chose not to mention his sister, perhaps the reason he lived as a recluse.

When she entered her bedchamber, she sighed. It was not a sigh of relief, but one of disappointment. She closed the door and placed her hands flat against the wood. Pressing her body up against it, she imagined what it would feel like if Gabriel held her against his muscular chest.

She tried to recall the first time she felt her body grow warm just from the sight of him and knew she had felt that way from the beginning. The feeling had grown in intensity. The first flicker of desire was now a blazing inferno, destined to destroy anything that got in its way.

The thud of boots making a slow ascent up the wooden staircase interrupted her reverie. They came to an abrupt halt at the far end of the landing. After a brief silence, she heard him walk towards her door.

Her heart hammered in her chest, her stomach fluttering from the thousand butterflies trapped inside. She could feel his presence as he hovered on the other side. Should she open the door? Should she invite him into her room, into her heart, into her bed?

While her mind moved frantically from one chaotic thought to another, she heard his steps recede, heard him open the door to his bedchamber and gently close it again.

The pain of loneliness was crippling. Rebecca closed her eyes and tried to remember how to breathe.

When she'd asked Gabriel if she could stay, her plea had been genuine—it was not seduction she had in mind. She thought of him as her friend, the only person in the world she could trust. If they crossed the line of propriety and became lovers, what would happen then?

Would he be her salvation or the cause of her ruination?

If George Wellford had his way, she would be married to a wealthy merchant by the end of the month, forced to spend the rest of her days in a cold, lifeless bed. The thought of what could have happened had she not fled the museum sent a terrifying shiver right through her.

Gabriel.

A burning need for him flooded her body with a heavenly feeling and she imagined a place where utter bliss was a certainty. In his arms, she could pander to her heart's desire, regardless of the consequences.

Pushing away from the door, she straightened her wrapper, moistened her lips and shook out her hair so it hung in waves about her shoulders.

She was strong-willed and fiercely independent. And she would have the man of her choosing, the only man she had ever wanted.

With her chin held high, she opened her door and walked with purposeful strides to stand outside his room. Taking a deep breath, she lifted her hand to knock. But before she knew what was happening, Gabriel yanked open the door, grabbed her by the wrist and pulled her inside.

Kicking the door shut with his boot, his gaze swept over her with a level of hunger that forced her to swallow. "Good God, woman, you'll be the death of me," he said as his mouth claimed hers in a passionate frenzy.

CHAPTER 14

*I*t felt as though he had waited a lifetime to kiss her again, had spent years wandering the dry, dusty desert searching for sustenance before stumbling upon a glittering oasis. The first taste of her lips sent ripples of pleasure flowing all the way down to his toes. And he drank in the intoxicating feeling in a bid to sate his thirst.

Out of desperation, he cradled her face and tilted her head, the angle making it easier to plunge his tongue deeper into her mouth, as he searched for a way to ease his torment. Her hot mouth welcomed his wild attack, and he dropped his hands, pulled her into an embrace in the hope of easing his throbbing cock.

Her trembling fingers edged up over his shoulders, and she sank them into his hair to pull him closer. The need to have her grew so fierce he wanted to throw his head back and howl. He wanted to rip and tear at her clothes and ravage her heavenly body.

"*Gabriel,*" she breathed, tilting her head to the side so he could kiss along the line of her jaw and down the perfect column of her neck.

That one word sang to him: *save me, show me, take me.* He knew if he did not rein in his rampant desire the memory of this night would be lost in a drunken blur.

Against the demands of his body, he broke contact and tried to calm his ragged breathing. "I do not have the strength to turn you away," he whispered, a little surprised his conscience had found a voice.

She put her hand on his cheek, and he leant into it. "I do not have the strength to run from it anymore, Gabriel. I cannot control what is happening to me. All I know is I need to be close to you." She glanced at the floor as a blush flooded her cheeks and when she looked up, her gaze appeared more purposeful. "I want to experience the physical bond between a man and a woman and I ... I want to experience it with you."

Her words were like a potent aphrodisiac, yet he could not define the feeling that swamped his mind and body: pure carnal lust fused with something else, something less tangible, but equally powerful.

With his gaze locked on hers, he pulled off his boots and then undid the ties on her wrapper, pushing it back off her shoulders until it fell to the floor. "Don't be afraid," he said, believing it was the right thing to say to a virgin.

Rebecca gave a little chuckle. "I am not afraid, Gabriel. Strangely, I have never felt more in control of anything my entire life."

Well, he would do everything he could to make her lose control.

"Good," he said, working on the knot in his cravat, "because I intend to worship your body, Rebecca. I intend to show you exactly how much I want you."

She stood there, in what he presumed was one of Mrs. Hudson's nightgowns, her generous breasts pushing against

ADELE CLEE

the confines of the fabric. Her wide eyes followed his movements with eager anticipation, the tip of her tongue touching her top lip as he yanked his shirt from his breeches and pulled it over his head.

Her gaze held a look of fascination as her hands came up to rest on his chest. The tips of her fingers traced the dusting of dark hair before wandering up over his shoulders and back down over the bulge of muscle in his upper arms.

He should have known she would not be shy and timid. He should have known her passionate nature would drive her to explore his body. It heightened his own pleasure to know he had the power to do this to her, that she wanted him and no other.

He unbuttoned his breeches, so they hung around his hips. "I seem to be at a disadvantage," he said as his gaze dropped to her white nightgown. "Here, allow me to rectify the problem."

Without protest, she lifted her arms in the air. He could tell from the glazed look in her eyes that she was already dizzy with desire. As he bunched the material up around her waist, his fingers brushed against her soft thighs, the movement inducing a tiny gasp of pleasure.

Gabriel thought he was a man of the world. He thought he had seen every beautiful sight there was to see.

He was wrong.

The sight of Rebecca standing before him, in all her naked glory, stole his breath away. Waves of rich copper curls hung wildly about milky-white skin. His palms itched at the sight of her full, round breasts, of her perky pink nipples, of her narrow waist flaring into curvaceous hips.

Bloody hell.

His mouth felt so dry he could hardly move his lips.

When he found the energy to step out of his breeches and drawers, his hard cock sprang free.

She glanced down and then her shocked gaze flew back to his face. He took her hand and pulled her into an embrace, sucking in a breath at the feel of her pliant body rubbing against him.

Brushing a tendril of hair from her face, he lowered his mouth to hers and kissed her with a slow, languorous grace that quickly became more passionate—more urgent.

It hit him then: the thought that he had never wanted anything as much as he wanted her.

Once would not be enough.

He feared he would never sate this delicious craving.

Kissing Gabriel felt so good Rebecca thought she might lose her mind.

It was the way his tongue danced with hers. The wild erotic dance made her feel breathless and dizzy—the deep thrusts forcing little gasps and moans.

She had no idea what to expect next. Yet she knew she was drowning in the depths of her own desire, carried along on wave after pleasurable wave that promised to deliver her to an idyllic shore.

Her body ached and throbbed but still she wanted more.

As though hearing her thoughts, Gabriel swung her up into his arms and carried her to the large four-poster, easing her down gently onto her back. He stood there for a moment, his greedy gaze devouring her body, lingering in the most intimate of places.

She should have felt embarrassed and self-conscious, but

she didn't. She felt wicked, desirable and needed. When his fingers trailed up over her thighs and across her stomach, she arched her back. The sensual movement made her breasts swell, made her nipples peak as a fiery heat pooled between her legs.

"I d-don't know what to do, Gabriel," she said, nerves pushing to the fore.

He moistened his lips. "You're doing perfectly well so far," he said, his voice a rich and heavy drawl. "Rest assured. If I die tonight, I shall die a happy man."

She had the power to do this to him, to make him swell with need, which despite her lack of experience gave her confidence in her ability as a woman.

"Make me happy, Gabriel," she said, offering her hand to him.

Make me forget all the lonely days and nights.

Gabriel took her hand and came down beside her onto the bed. The sheer size of him, coupled with the heat radiating from his skin, caused a throbbing between her legs that cried out for his touch.

He took her mouth more gently this time, his tongue tracing the line of her lips as though relishing the taste. When their tongues met, she heard a pleasurable hum resonate from the back of his throat. It was a sound she wanted to hear again, and it spurred her on to be a little bolder.

As she pressed her body to his, he moaned as his hard length rubbed against her stomach. He kissed her neck, her breasts, teasing her nipple with his tongue and she felt a pulsating deep in her core. He trailed kisses down to her stomach, kissing and nipping at her inner thigh, between her legs. Before she could catch her breath, his wicked tongue sucked and licked the tiny bud there, until she felt the coil inside wind tighter and tighter, until her world exploded in a dazzling ray of glittering lights.

Pleasure burst forth in powerful waves. The tremors carrying a rush of pure emotion for the man who was slowly working his way back up to her.

"You're sure about this?" he panted, positioning himself between her thighs, his devilish grin melting her heart. "It's not too late to change your mind."

Change her mind?

"I'm sure," she whispered, her head still floating in the clouds.

There was nothing she wanted more.

"Thank God, as I cannot wait a moment longer. There is no easy way to do this, but I promise you it will not be uncomfortable for long."

She nodded as she caressed his back and shoulders, lifted her mouth to his to show she wanted him, regardless. Despite the discomfort, she welcomed the intrusion as he entered her.

"*Rebecca*," he whispered as he pushed deeper. And as she stretched to fit him, the look on his face suggested he adored the feel of her.

He kissed her then, their tongues tangling with a rampant need, the hair on his chest brushing against her sensitive nipples as he pushed through her maidenhead, swallowing down her tiny shriek, making her forget it should feel anything other than divine.

Together they found their rhythm, rocking in unison, driving closer and closer to the blissful peak of their passion.

She could feel him moving inside her. Filling her, completing her, chasing away every lonely thought she'd ever had, and she didn't want it to end. Her frantic hands clawed at the muscles in his back, scrambled lower to dig into his buttocks, to spur him on. Every part of her was made to fit with him. She clung on, anchoring him to her body, to her soul, as his thrusts became more desperate, harder and more frantic.

The feeling was upon her again. It started in the pit of her stomach, pooling and pulsating between her thighs, the waves of pleasure shooting down to her toes as her body sang to his tune.

"*Oh, Gabriel, I ... I.*"

"*Rebecca.*"

Her breathless pants mingled with his guttural groans. She felt the muscles in his legs stiffen, heard his roar of satisfaction as she soared through some imaginary heaven.

When their breathing slowed, he looked down at her, his gaze warm and tender and he lowered his head and kissed her softly on the mouth before collapsing in an exhausted heap.

As he lay sprawled across her, his back damp from over-exertion, his eyes closed in sated slumber, she knew he had not only claimed her body. He had claimed her heart and soul, too. And as she closed her eyes to join him in sleep, she did so in the blissful knowledge that she had fallen in love with Gabriel Stone.

CHAPTER 15

*G*abriel woke from the wild, passionate dream to find a warm, feminine body curled next to him.

He felt her slender thigh draped over his leg, her hand splayed over his chest covering his heart, her breasts squashed against his ribs. In her slumber, her breath tickled the hair on his chest like a gentle breeze. He had never felt so sated, so content. Yet somewhere deep inside, the desperate ache for her still gnawed away, and he knew he would take her again.

He would take her now if the opportunity presented itself.

Gabriel could not remember another time in his life when he'd acted so recklessly. To take an unmarried lady as a lover was scandalous. To take the daughter of an old friend was sinful. Falling prey to the weakness of his own desire was an entirely new experience.

As his mind replayed a series of lascivious images, a recount of their amorous encounter that did little to ease the ache between his legs, *reckless* did not even begin to describe his conduct.

Lost in the dizzying heights of his own release, he had forgotten to withdraw.

Bloody hell.

But that was not his only *faux pas*.

What sort of gentleman takes a lady's virginity, collapses on top of her and then promptly falls asleep? Next time he would be more alert, more attentive. He would not be so damn careless.

Would there be a next time?

The question bounced back and forth in his mind, challenging him for an answer before he settled on—definitely. Despite every foolish and sinful thing he'd done, the thought that he would never have her again, never taste her sweet mouth, never experience such bone-shattering satisfaction, was impossible to comprehend.

Even now, he had to fight the irresistible urge to roll on top of her and bury himself deep inside, the snug fit so deliciously tempting. Instead, he did something he knew he would regret. He gathered her closer to his chest, caressed her back with soothing strokes and tried to understand what the hell was happening to him.

He had sworn never to let anyone get this close.

So why did he persistently ignore his own advice? Gabriel had known her for four days, yet it felt as though he had known her a lifetime. The thought unsettled him. If he felt this way now, how would he feel after a month?

Needing a distraction, he eased her out of his grip and climbed out of bed. The room felt cold. And so he pulled the sheets over her naked body, swallowing down his desire as he did so, promptly throwing on his shirt and breeches.

It was strange how comfortable he felt having her in his private chamber. His house was his sanctuary, the only place he felt at peace. No other woman had eased her way into his heart. No other woman had found the secret door to his soul.

Dipping his fingers into the washbowl, he splashed his face with cold water. The water he should have used to wash away the evidence of his release.

Then another thought struck him—there would have been blood.

He hadn't even bothered to ask if she'd experienced any discomfort. He hadn't taken the time to show her that his feelings ran deeper than the need for carnal gratification.

"You're awake early."

Her voice sounded deep and languid from sleep, an erotic blend that spoke to his primal needs. Yet when he turned to face her, it was his heart that swelled.

"I appear to have fallen asleep somewhat prematurely last night," he said, walking over to sit on the bed, dismissing the fact the sensations in his chest were new to him. "The least I can do is arrange breakfast."

"Last night? Gabriel, it was a few hours ago." She sat upright, holding the sheet under her arms to keep it in place, although the sight of her bare shoulders was enough to rouse his manhood to attention.

Gabriel had never taken a woman's virginity. He had never dealt with the slight awkwardness, with the feeling of wanting to ask intimate questions, but not really knowing how to broach the subject. "Are you all right? After this morning, I mean."

The words sounded childish and pathetic, but Rebecca's smile made the world seem a brighter place.

"I'm fine," she said, her cheeks flushing pink. "It was, well, it was everything I thought it would be."

His masculine pride could not help but ask, "In a good way?"

"Of course in a good way," she said with a chuckle. "In an extremely good way."

Relief flashed through him. "Are you hungry?"

"Ravenous."

"Perhaps it would be better if we dressed and then ate downstairs." He did not want his staff to discover Rebecca in his room, but that was not the only reason. A comfortable familiarity clung to him, making him forget to build his barricade, making him feel bare and exposed.

"I'm afraid the best I can do is an itchy nightdress and a wrapper," she said, glancing around the room. "They're here somewhere."

"Well, a nightdress is slightly more appropriate than your current state of undress." He considered jumping back into bed and taking the only sustenance he needed. But he mentally chastised himself for the inability to think of anything other than salacious thoughts. "I shall have some fresh water sent to your bedchamber and meet you in the dining room in thirty minutes. It will also give you a moment to think about how you want to proceed." When she looked a little startled, he added, "You cannot go home, Rebecca. At least not yet."

She stared at him for a moment. "We will discuss it over breakfast," she said with a certain finality, which meant she had already made up her mind.

When he found the courage to tell her about the painting, perhaps she would view things differently.

The thought caused him to swallow deeply.

"Very well." He nodded as he turned to the door, his weakened position leaving him unprepared for her next question.

"I haven't had a chance to ask you before," she said, calling out to him, "but I wondered why you never mentioned you had a sister? I assume she lives with her mother."

Gabriel froze.

The words were said so casually, yet they struck him like a vicious blow. He struggled to turn around and face her, fearing she would see the truth in his eyes. The ridiculous truth—that he blamed them for something, for nothing, for everything.

"We are estranged," he said coldly. "I provide for them financially, but keep my distance for reasons I do not care to go into."

Lord knows what she was thinking. Fearing another verbal assault, another prying attack, he made his escape in the guise of needing to locate Mrs. Hudson.

As he made his way downstairs, the past weighed heavily on his shoulders. Having Rebecca in the house, seeing her snuggled in his bed, the honest discussions, the comfortable breakfast, all made it feel less like an institute for research, less like a haven for scholars and more like a family home.

The words *family* and *home* caused panic to flare.

A home should be a place of affection and security. He knew it as a place where deception lay hidden amongst the fake smiles and caring gestures. A place tarnished and dirty, a place of pain and anguish and he had sworn never to put himself in such a predicament again.

For his own sanity, for his own protection, Rebecca Linwood could not stay another night in his house.

Rebecca felt ridiculous sitting in a formal dining room in her nightclothes while Gabriel sat dressed in a navy-blue coat and beige breeches. The staff made no mention of the fact and busied about her as though she were mistress of the house and could do as she pleased.

Gabriel, on the other hand, had eaten half of his meal without saying a word.

The atmosphere brimmed with suppressed tension, as though he had stuffed his feelings into a chest and been forced to sit on the lid to stop them from leaping out.

In mentioning his sister, had she roused painful memories of the past?

Or was it her presence he found stifling?

The life of a recluse demanded peace and solitude. Perhaps he struggled with the idea that someone else was invading his personal space. After all, she'd turned his world on its head in the last few days, and he had a habit of withdrawing into himself, of putting up a blockade to prevent anyone from entering. She had seen it at George Wellford's house, and she could see it now.

Perhaps he wanted her in his bed but did not need her troubles and complications in his life.

With a heavy heart, she said, "Thank you for letting me stay last night. But I think it best I go home after breakfast."

When he looked up, she diverted her gaze, feigning interest in the eggs on her plate.

"I thought we had already established that is not possible."

"Well, I cannot stay here," she said, testing the theory that he would be pleased to have the house to himself again. When he failed to reply, he confirmed her suspicion, and the thought reinforced the dull ache in her chest.

He put down his cutlery, wiped his mouth with his napkin and gave a deep sigh. "There is something I need to tell you. Something—" He stopped abruptly and swallowed before speaking again. "Something happened at your house last night."

She felt the blood drain from her face, pooling in her throat, thick and heavy. Something terrible had happened, and he'd kept it from her. "What is it? What happened? Did you lie about my father's things?"

Gabriel shook his head. "No, I did not lie to you, Rebecca." His tone suggested a disdain for lies and untruths, suggested the words were abhorrent and the remark offended him. "An item was damaged, ruined, but not one of the antiquities."

Her hand flew to her chest desperate to ease the pounding. "Not one of the paintings in the lower gallery?" Heaven help her. She would have to sell her soul to cover the cost. "They're on loan, Gabriel, and I don't have the money to replace them."

He pursed his lips, closed his eyes briefly. She knew that whatever he was going to say would hurt her. "It's the painting, the one of your mother. When I got there, I found it on the chair. Someone slashed the canvas with a knife. Whoever defaced it wanted it to be the first thing you saw when you walked into the room."

She repeated his words in her head, praying she'd misheard. But bile erupted in her stomach and threatened to rise up to burn the back of her throat. Who would do such a thing? Who despised her so much that they could rip out her heart for their own pleasure?

As she struggled to speak, only one word escaped from her lips. "Why?"

Gabriel brushed his hand through his hair: a sign of anger, frustration or guilt, she didn't know. "I wanted to tell you last night. I should have told you last night."

Her painting destroyed ... her mother gone.

She stared straight through him, not really listening. His words were one long mumbling sound. Rational thought tried to break through her chaotic emotions. It was only a painting. Yet the pain that choked her and robbed her of her breath felt as raw as the day her mother died.

Transported back to the gloomy room, she thought of the moment her mother took her last breath, the moment she felt the huge gaping hole open in her chest. Now the hole had been torn open anew.

It's only a painting.

The faint words drifted through her mind again. It was more than a painting to her. The angelic face acted as a constant reminder that the house had once been filled with love. It watched over her, providing comfort and companion-ship and the strength to strive forward each day.

Now, like all the other good things in her life, it was gone.

How long would it be before she lost Gabriel?

She stood abruptly, the chair scraping against the wooden floor. Gabriel stood, too.

"I'm sorry, Rebecca. I know what it means to you. I'm sure it can be repaired. There is an artist ..."

He continued talking, but she stopped listening.

A few hours ago, she had experienced one moment of sheer bliss. A moment of freedom from all the pain and disap-pointment. But the new day had brought with it the reality of the situation: she was one of those unfortunate people who attracted nothing but hurt and suffering. It was only a matter of time before the beauty of the man before her turned into something sour, before it turned into something that made her heart ache with sadness, not joy.

A sob caught in the back of her throat.

Loving Gabriel had created a new wound. One that she suspected would never heal.

"I must go," she said, trying not to look at him for fear of melting under his sinful gaze, suddenly grateful for the solid table standing between them. "Would you mind sending for your carriage? And I will need my cloak."

He gave an exasperated sigh. "Then I shall accompany you."

"No!" The word came out as a shriek. "I'll be fine. Mrs. James will be there and Mr. Pearce. I ... I would like to rest in my quarters. I would like to be alone." She felt weak and nauseous and being alone was a feeling she knew how to deal with, a feeling she lived with daily.

Gabriel cursed and muttered to himself. "Then let Higson accompany you. He can repair the basement door while you rest." His voice sounded strained, but she could not worry about that.

She agreed and waited for him to leave the room. She waited until the sound of his boots echoed down the hallway and then exhaled, releasing years of suppressed pain, hugged her stomach and let the tears fall.

CHAPTER 16

*R*ebecca felt exhausted and emotional, yet the rhythmical rocking of the carriage did little to soothe her spirit.

A hint of cedar hung in the air. The smell reminded her of Gabriel's skin, of his hair and his mouth. The carriage felt like a dark void: cold and empty without him in it.

As they rumbled out of Hanover Square, she forced her gaze to her lap, knowing that to see Gabriel's solemn face would tear at her heart, and she could not think about that, not today.

It was almost eleven o'clock when they rolled into Coventry Street, the high sun visible as the street bustled with activity. Dogs chased after their master's heels. Ladies strolled in groups displaying their pretty parasols, a man dodging them as he navigated the crowd while balancing paper parcels on his head. The world was blissfully unaware of the sadness consuming her.

When they pulled up outside her house, Higson jumped down and advised her to wait in the carriage while he went inside to find the housekeeper.

Visitors eager to experience the wonders of Egypt queued at the front door. The proprietor wearing nothing but a night-gown and a damp silk cloak was not on the list of recommended attractions.

Higson returned with a pale blue pelisse and matching parasol and waited while Rebecca made herself look more respectable before escorting her into the house.

"I'll go and see about the basement door," he said, seeing her safely to the third floor. "And I'll report back before I leave."

Rebecca nodded.

Clutching the folded parasol like a weapon, she walked towards the parlour. Holding her breath, she anticipated seeing the damaged portrait for the first time. She winced, fearing one glance would scorch her eyes.

However, the painting was not on the chair as Gabriel had mentioned.

"Higson," she called out to the coachman. He plodded back up the stairs and crossed the landing to stand in front of her. Upon closer inspection, his thick side-whiskers made his face seem fuller, friendlier than she expected. His warm countenance was so opposed to his hulking frame. "Last night, you were with Mr. Stone when he checked the building."

"Aye, I was, miss."

"He told me the damaged painting had been left on the chair." Rebecca pointed to where she expected to find the memory of her mother torn to tatters.

Higson lifted his chin, gesturing to the empty chair. "Mr. Stone moved it. He didn't want to cause any more distress than was necessary."

"I see."

It was a thoughtful gesture. Whoever left it there wanted

her to see it in all its wicked glory, shredded and maimed, the soul stripped out.

"He put it behind the chair," Higson said, holding out a meaty finger to direct her gaze.

Rebecca shook her head when she noticed the corners of the gilt frame poking out at the sides. She stared at the decorative edges, fear growing in her chest as she anticipated the pain she knew would follow.

"It feels as though my mother's memory has been desecrated. It feels as though she has died all over again." She hadn't meant to say the words aloud. Higson glanced behind to see if she was talking to someone else. "How could anyone be so cruel?"

"If you don't mind me saying, miss. All the precious things are in our head. Memories, that's what counts. There's no need for objects when your memory serves you well enough."

Rebecca stared at him, his words filtering through all the madness. "Memories are painful, Higson. Objects have a way of making us feel connected to the person."

"I don't follow, miss." Higson scratched his temple. "What need is there for objects when our loved ones never truly leave us? How can they when they're in our hearts? No one can rip the love from our hearts. No one can destroy the memories in our head."

Rebecca felt a sudden rush of compassion as she knew Higson spoke from experience. "You speak like a man who has lost a loved one. Like a man who has suffered the loss of a parent."

The corners of his mouth turned downward, and he sighed. "Not a parent. I never knew them. It was a wife I lost."

The harrowing image of Gabriel lying cold on a stone

slab caused her heart to hammer against her ribs. "I … I am sorry, Higson. I can only imagine how difficult it must have been."

"Pay it no heed, miss. It was a long time ago. Daresay the heart never truly heals. But like I said, everything I need to know is stored in my head."

Rebecca forced a smile. Would she ever feel that level of acceptance? Did she really need to surround herself with her parents' belongings to keep their memory alive?

"I think I have formed attachments to things, to objects, as though they contain the essence of the person, if that makes any sense. I feel the same way about my father's relics as I do my mother's painting." She had no idea why she was telling Gabriel's coachman her innermost thoughts. Perhaps it was because he was easy to talk to. Indeed, he did not judge her and her heart didn't flutter when she looked into his eyes. "Being around their things gives me purpose."

Higson's expression softened. "I know it's not my place to say, but when you only take comfort from the past, then there's no hope for the future. I don't suppose that's what your parents would have wanted."

The man was wiser than his years and his station.

"It's the same for Mr. Stone," he continued with a shrug. "But that's his story to tell."

A hundred questions flooded her mind. "Does Mr. Stone ever talk about his sister?" she asked, even though she knew Higson would never betray a trust. Besides, she suspected Gabriel never spoke about his feelings to anyone.

"Not to me, miss."

"Thank you, Higson. You have been a great help today. More than you know."

His plump face flushed, and he shuffled from side to side while standing on the same spot. "I'd best go down and look at that door. Mr. Stone won't be happy until he knows you're safe."

The last comment caused a bolt of awareness to shoot through her, an intense desire to feel encased in the strong arms of his master—the only place she truly felt safe.

Higson walked out into the hall, but then stopped and with a deep sigh trudged back to stand in the doorway.

"About Mr. Stone," he said with a slight tremor in his voice. "He needs you, miss. He needs you more than he's needed anything his whole life. He's not the easiest of gentlemen, I know, but I once heard it said that the rocky path always has the better view." Higson tipped an invisible hat and stalked off down the stairs.

Rebecca stood in frozen silence as she watched him go.

He needs you more than he's needed anything his whole life.

The words echoed in her mind, filling her with a sense of purpose, flooding her body with warm feelings of desire, of love, of a longing that burned with such vibrant intensity.

No one had ever needed her.

No one could imagine how desperately she wanted those words to be true. How they penetrated the loneliness, banishing it back to its cold dark place.

When you only take comfort from the past, then there's no hope for the future.

Drawing strength from Higson's wise words, she walked over to the chair and dragged the painting out to examine the damage.

Holding back a surge of emotion, she noticed there were two diagonal slashes across the canvas. They split her mother's perfect face into four equal triangles, each piece flapping back and forth. It was a despicable thing for anyone to do and an hour earlier she would have sobbed until there were no more tears left to shed.

With a deep breath and a renewed sense of optimism, she pressed the pieces back into place. As the face became whole again, she noticed her mother was still smiling.

Higson was right.

Nothing could erase the memory of her mother's happy countenance. To Rebecca, she would always be smiling, and she did not need a painting to remind her of that.

With a full heart, a feeling she thought she'd never experience again once witnessing the damage, she gathered the strength to hang it back on the wall above the fireplace. It would stay there until she got it repaired. It would remind her that love lived in her heart.

Rebecca spent a few minutes looking at the portrait, letting only positive memories of love and affection fill her thoughts. Grief had a way of numbing all other emotions, and she did not want to live her life in a state of constant sorrow.

By some miracle, she had found the one person who made the future appear brighter. She had fallen in love with Gabriel Stone, with the charismatic scholar of Egyptology whose intense passion often robbed her of her breath. When she thought of him, her heart soared. She would not run away from her feelings. She would not let the fear of loss influence any future decisions.

What was Gabriel's story?

Higson had suggested a similarity to her own. If so, Rebecca would help him to look beyond his grief. If he came to her, which she hoped he would, she would do everything in her power to show him that a life and a future existed beyond the pain of the past.

CHAPTER 17

*G*abriel milled about the house for hours, wandering from room to room, feigning interest in his books, in a piece of plum tart and a broken eyeglass, in anything that would stop him thinking about the events of the morning.

It was no good, he thought, throwing himself down on the sofa. He had to address his feelings at some point. He could not walk about in this comatose state for the rest of his life.

It was time to acknowledge the fact that he had stood like a dimwit, a man robbed of all sense and logic, and watched Rebecca leave. A tiny part of him had breathed a sigh of relief. Her absence gave him time to reflect, time to repair and reinforce his defensive wall. The largest part of him felt like a drunken sot who had lost his entire fortune in one idiotic turn of the dice. The lesson being, one should never play games with those things considered most precious.

You are not the man I hoped you would be.

She had used those words at their first meeting, and perhaps she was right.

He could be a friend and a lover.

But never anything more.

Never a husband.

He had been deliberately quiet at breakfast, rudely so, withdrawn even, lost in some fearful nightmare from the past. Rebecca had sat dressed in the cotton nightdress, the one he'd so eagerly dragged over her head just a few hours before, eating toast and sipping tea. He half expected the door to burst open and the room to explode with the bustling sound of hungry children. Their children, all sharing breakfast in their family home.

And it scared the hell out of him.

The comfortable scene reminded him of a time in his youth. He had come down to take breakfast with his father, his mother's chair cold and empty at the end of the table. Perhaps his father thought a mouthful of eggs rendered the news of his upcoming nuptials less shocking. Like a startled deer, Gabriel's gaze had shot to the empty chair. Sitting in silence, he counted the weeks since his mother's passing. Yet he knew it was only seven.

The talk in the servants' quarters was that his father had been desperate for an opportunity to remarry. Indeed, a new mother soon followed and then a sibling. The irony being that he had never felt more alone in his entire life.

Loneliness consumed him. It drove him to form an obsession with Egypt. He mirrored himself on his mentor, Lord Wellford, believing him the epitome of everything a man should be: loyal, devoted and honest.

Even that turned out to be a lie.

He still felt a thread of vengeance running through his veins. His heart was torn between a genuine sadness for Rebecca's plight and wishing he could slash and stab at a painting of his own stepmother. Wishing he could hurt his sister the way her mother and father had hurt him.

That's why he stayed away: because of the guilt, anger and shame.

There were many similarities between his situation and Rebecca's. So many, he could not help but feel that fate had conspired to throw them together, and these strange coincidences were not coincidental at all.

Perhaps in understanding his own disgraceful feelings, it would help him to discover who wanted to hurt Rebecca.

The answer was obvious. The only people with motive were the Wellfords.

He recalled the three brothers: George, Alexander and Frederick. They all had a reason to hate her, more reason to hate than even he could comprehend. Their mother had lived to witness her husband's indiscretion.

Rebecca's safety was of paramount concern and despite her plea for secrecy, Gabriel decided he would begin by calling on George Wellford.

Gabriel rode halfway across town only to discover that Lord Wellford had gone to his club. In his current mood, he did not want to wait until Wellford returned home and so swallowed down the feeling of irritation, dismissed his anxiety at having to mingle amongst the elite of Society.

The look of surprise on the faces of the gentlemen who acknowledged him with a respectful nod reflected his own shock at being there.

Thankfully, Wellford sat alone, next to the white marble fireplace, a copy of the *Times* in one hand and a glass of port in the other. A steward approached. Wellford put down his drink and newspaper, his inquisitive gaze drifting beyond the man's shoulder, locking with Gabriel's frustrated glare.

Wellford beckoned him over. "Won't you join me, Stone?" He gestured to the empty chair. "I'm ordering luncheon if you're hungry."

Gabriel did not intend to stay long. The pale-green walls were supposed to be calming, but they would need to plunge him into a vat of it to achieve the desired effect. "No, thank you. But I will have a pot of coffee."

Wellford relayed the order to the steward and waited for him to depart. "I did not know you were a member," he said in a lofty tone. "I assume you're looking for me."

"I am, and I've been a member for years." It was not out of choice. His uncle insisted on securing membership for all the gentlemen in the family. This was the first time it had proved useful.

"Then sit."

Gabriel pulled the chair out and sat down. "Does being a member mean I'm now on your list of respectable gentlemen?"

The corners of Wellford's mouth turned up into a half smile. "Have you come to declare your intentions?"

"There is nothing to declare." He shrugged. "I had the utmost respect for your father, and I offer his daughter the same courtesy. What more do you want me to say?" It was not a lie, and so he could accept the fact it was not entirely the whole truth.

Wellford leant forward. "Look, I was angry when I insulted you. I'm sure your intentions towards Rebecca are respectable. Besides, last night you had the look of a man obsessed, besotted. Now you have the look of a man in love. Forgive me if I jumped to conclusions."

Gabriel snorted. He was a man in lust, a man ravaged by the needs of his body. There was a vast difference. He could not deny that his affections were engaged, but it would not be fair to either of them to allow it to develop into anything deeper.

"You have a right to your opinion, but that's not why I'm here."

The steward returned with their drinks and Gabriel informed him he would pour his own coffee, much to the man's chagrin.

"Men like to earn their wages, Stone," Wellford said once the steward moved out of earshot. "If everyone poured their own drinks, the man would be out of a job."

Gabriel did not need a lecture on etiquette. "Forgive me if I lack the refinement necessary to lounge about at my club all day, waiting for the staff to wipe my nose."

Rather than appear offended, Wellford chuckled. "Are we to share barbed insults for the rest of the afternoon? Don't despise me for being concerned about my sister."

"Don't despise *me* for being concerned about your sister." Gabriel knew he was provoking the man, but he couldn't help himself.

Wellford relaxed back in his chair. "Look, let us draw a line and begin again. You obviously see more of Rebecca than I do. It appeases my conscience to know someone is looking out for her, in a *brotherly* way."

There was a hint of sarcasm as he stressed those last few words. Deliberate or not, it caused guilt to flare in Gabriel's chest.

"Why do you even care what happens to her?" Gabriel sneered. The question was blunt and to the point, revealing an inner frustration and Wellford reeled from the shock.

"She's my sister," he said, making a quick recovery. "Why would I not care about her?"

"Because she reminds you of your father's indiscretion." There, he'd said it and could not take it back now. "Do your brothers feel the same way as you do?"

Wellford shrugged, choosing not to address the first

comment. "I assume so, yes. What is this all about, Stone? I came here for peace and relaxation not for you to drag me over hot coals for some unknown transgression."

Against his own counsel and because he thought it would help determine who wanted to hurt Rebecca, Gabriel revealed something he had always kept secret.

"When my mother died, my father remarried quickly. I despised him for it because I felt he'd disrespected her memory. I despised my stepmother and chose to pretend that my sister did not exist. Your father's indiscretion was deemed far worse."

Gabriel saw a flicker of uncertainty in Wellford's confident gaze. "I suppose you think one truth deserves another."

"Isn't that the way it works?"

Wellford reached for his glass and swallowed what was left of his port. "My father's actions were unforgivable. After Rebecca's birth, my mother was never the same again. She died of a broken heart years before her body grew cold. Love does strange things to men as I am sure you will agree. But I have come to terms with my parents' weaknesses and have decided to respect the wishes of my father by protecting the daughter he loved."

"Rebecca believes your interest lies in the museum. That she is an embarrassment to your family, and you want rid of her."

Wellford gave a mocking snort. "My father was unfaithful to his family long before he met Rebecca's mother. His work was his mistress, and we all suffered greatly for it. Why would I want to be reminded that he worshipped the dead over the living?"

An unsettling thought entered Gabriel's head, a recognition that his work was his mistress, too, and he preferred the dead to the living. "Is she an embarrassment to you?" he asked, focusing his frustration elsewhere.

Wellford snorted and shook his head. "No, she is not an embarrassment. Would I have escorted her out amongst Society if she were? I want her to marry, to have protection and security. I want her to have the respect she deserves and not be judged for my father's mistakes. That is all."

Gabriel took a sip of coffee in the hope the warm liquid would soothe his agitated mind.

Was he guilty of judging his own sister for their father's mistake? Why were the unrealistic expectations of his childhood still plaguing him now?

With a quick shake of the head, he pushed the thoughts far from his mind and focused on the anger he knew would resurface with his next comment. "Two men broke into Rebecca's house last night and used a knife to slash the painting of her mother. Thankfully, she escaped before anything untoward happened."

Wellford almost shot out of the chair. "What the hell," he whispered, yet the words conveyed vehemence. "Was she hurt? Where is she now?"

She was at the museum as he had been stupid enough to let her leave without him.

"She's fine," he said in an attempt to convince himself. "Naturally, she is upset but insisted on returning to the museum. My man Higson is with her for the time being."

Wellford's eyes widened. "She's gone back to the museum? Heavens above, I have never known a woman so stubborn."

"In that, we are agreed," he said, remembering how she refused to move from his front steps. Remembering how her tenacity made him hard with need. "Do you happen to know where your brothers were last night?"

"Alex and Freddie?" he replied in a tone of disbelief. "Surely you don't think they had anything to do with it?"

"They have a motive." Gabriel shrugged. "Who else would ignore valuable antiquities to destroy a painting?" *Only someone out for vengeance*, he added silently.

Wellford fell quiet for a moment. "Alexander is in Italy. He dreams of being a great painter and has been away for months. Freddie was probably so inebriated he slept in his clothes. I will speak to him this evening."

"Rebecca will not take kindly to your involvement, so it is best if you refrain from charging over there making ridiculous demands."

"Well, you can't expect me just to sit back and do nothing."

Gabriel winced, knowing Wellford would be furious with his next suggestion. "Then you will have to trust me because if I cannot persuade Rebecca to leave the museum, I will be forced to stay there with her."

Wellford did shoot out of his seat. "Like hell you will."

"Sit down. You'll make yourself ill if you keep jumping up like that."

Wellford flopped back down into the chair. "It occurs to me that this is all very convenient. Maybe you slashed the painting as a ploy to get close to her."

Gabriel suppressed a look of guilt as he recalled how deliciously close they had been last night. "I shall pretend I didn't hear that. Rebecca trusts no one. My only concern is keeping her safe, her reputation unblemished. She lives in an Egyptian museum for heaven's sake. A hundred people must pass through there every day. No one will notice me entering."

Wellford stared at him, his gaze intrusive, assessing.

"It was my idea to seek you out," Gabriel added. "I wanted to be honest with you, to ask for your support."

A faint smile touched the corners of Wellford's mouth. "What choice do I have? Rebecca will refuse to see me, and I cannot leave her alone. So I am forced to concede. I concede because I believe you're in love with her. And because your involvement has dragged you out of your Egyptian tomb, out into the daylight. I am hoping your influence will encourage her to do the same. Perhaps you could take her to Vauxhall or riding in the park. My father trusted you, Stone, and so I am trusting you."

The words cut deep as Gabriel had already abused his trust, already fallen foul to temptation, to the weaknesses of the flesh and so all he could manage in reply was, "Thank you."

"However, I ask one thing in return." Wellford's tone had grown more solemn now.

"I can hardly wait to hear it."

"Should anything untoward happen, I want your assurance, as a gentleman, that you'll marry her."

All the air suddenly escaped from Gabriel's lungs. "Marry her?" he repeated as the words *family*, *home* and *marriage* pecked away at him like the crow of death.

How could he make such an oath when he'd sworn he would never marry? How could he agree to marriage when he believed it to be an institution for deception?

He was overreacting. Nothing would go wrong. As a partner in the museum, his presence could be easily explained. "I give you my word. I will make her an offer, but I cannot guarantee Rebecca will accept."

Wellford chucked. "I am astounded that a man of your intelligence cannot see what is right in front of his nose. I trust you to protect Rebecca and, in the meantime, I will go in search of Freddie and will inform you should anything arise."

Gabriel stood and offered a respectful bow.

"Won't you at least stay and finish your coffee?"

Gabriel shook his head. He would feel safer in a cage of starving lions. "If my uncle finds me here, I will be bombarded with invitations for the next six months. He will hound me until I am forced to bury myself away in my tomb and scratch a curse on the door."

Wellford laughed. "Then I suggest you run. I have it on good authority that there is no such thing as curses."

CHAPTER 18

*G*abriel sat behind his desk, flipped open the ledger and checked the columns for the fifth time. If only he could stumble upon a mistake, a grave error to occupy his mind and reinforce the feeling that his house was nothing but an institute, an emotionless vessel for his studies.

He heard Higson's heavy gait trudge along the hallway and his thoughts flew back to Rebecca, his stomach performing somersaults at the prospect of seeing her again.

Pushing his hand through his hair, he took a deep breath, mentally preparing himself for the tears that would inevitably accompany any conversation involving the painting.

Higson rapped on the open door and stepped over the threshold. "I'm all done at the museum. The basement door's been fixed and is secure like you asked."

Gabriel's gaze drifted beyond the man's shoulder to the empty space behind him, to where he expected to see his flame-haired temptress with her luscious lips and sultry smile. Disappointment flared in his chest.

"How is Miss Linwood?" he said, batting down the need to ask why the hell she was still at the museum.

Higson shrugged. "I think she's bearing up under the circumstances."

The man was as free with his information as he was his emotion.

"I assume she's upset."

Thankfully, Higson's answer amounted to more than a few words, although the cryptic response proved just as frustrating. "The problem is, she looks on her possessions as though they are living things. She said it feels like her mother has died all over again."

Guilt twisted its knife into Gabriel's heart. He should not have let her go alone. He should have been there to offer support.

"I left her in the storeroom, sorting through some wooden crates," Higson continued, "sending that curator of hers running here, there and everywhere doing her bidding."

A sense of relief should have swamped him. At least she'd not taken to her bed consumed with grief. Yet he could not help but be plagued by thoughts of his own inadequacy, by the uncomfortable feeling that she didn't need him.

"Did she not ask to return here with you?"

"She never mentioned it, and I never asked. She seemed right enough to me."

Gabriel struggled to hide his frustration. "Thank you, Higson. You may return to your duties. I won't need the carriage again today."

What was he supposed to do now?

Should he just sit and wait for her to knock on his door in the dead of night? Should he try to push aside the image of a mysterious intruder attacking her in her bed?

Forcing himself from the chair, he paced the room, waiting for the answer to pop into his head. He could not leave her alone there, and so had no option but to visit her in Coventry Street.

The clock on the mantel chimed three.

If he left now, no one would question him entering her house. He would just be another visitor to the museum. If he took one or two small antiquities, he could continue with the charade of being a partner in the business. At the museum, they were less at risk of causing a scandal—and no scandal meant no marriage.

Some thirty minutes later, parcel in hand, he made his way on foot, walking down through Swallow Street and onto Piccadilly as that was the quickest route.

By the time he arrived at the museum, there were still a dozen people perusing the exhibits.

Gabriel spotted Mr. Pearce explaining the history of the stone tablets to a few who had gathered around to listen. He waited for the group to depart before calling out to the curator. "Mr. Pearce, a moment of your time, if you please."

The man scurried over to meet him, his eyes flitting about in their sockets, moving left and right, up and down before settling on Gabriel's chin.

"I have brought a few antiquities to display," Gabriel said, gesturing to the parcel. "Is Miss Linwood home?" It was not really a question as he presumed to know the answer.

"No, Mr. Stone. Miss Linwood has gone out."

"Out?" He had not thought to say the word aloud but supposed it was better than saying, "Where the hell has she gone?"

"Yes." Mr. Pearce nodded, wringing his hands as he struggled to make eye contact. "She went shopping about an hour ago."

"Shopping? On her own?"

Mr. Pearce looked confused. "Miss Linwood always goes out unaccompanied."

Gabriel shook his head. The woman's logic confounded him at every turn. Was she not the least bit worried about the men who had broken into her home? Those same men could be trailing behind her while she ran her errands.

Then a sudden feeling of apprehension flashed through him.

Perhaps she had gone to see George Wellford, to berate him over the damaged painting. What if Wellford told her about their earlier discussion, where he had said he would act as chaperone, where he said he would marry her should any problems arise?

Pushing the thoughts aside and with a frustrated sigh, he said, "Very well, I shall wait for her in the office."

Mr. Pearce bowed, and as he moved to walk away, Gabriel called him back. "Despite Miss Linwood's leniency with regard to your disgraceful conduct, I want you to know I am not as forgiving."

Mr. Pearce's thin lips disappeared even further into his mouth.

"Your opinion, or Lord Wellford's for that matter, is of no concern," Gabriel continued. "In future, I expect you to treat Miss Linwood with the respect she deserves."

Mr. Pearce offered no excuse for his crime. "I understand, sir," he said with a solemn bow before walking away.

Gabriel wandered down to the office. It felt awkward entering Rebecca's private space, uninvited. His gaze drifted beyond the crude wooden chair to the small sofa. The red damask covers were worn and threadbare in places, but it looked comfortable enough. So he unbuttoned his coat, brushed the seat to remove the fine layer of dust and settled down to wait.

When the clock chimed four, Gabriel closed his eyes. Suffering from a distinct lack of sleep, thanks to the passionate Miss Linwood, he decided to take a nap.

But peace eluded him, driven away by the recurring *ding dong* ringing out every fifteen minutes. He thought he would grow accustomed to the sound, yet found himself glancing up at the clock, counting each slow revolution until it chimed five. By the time the hands approached six, he was restless, impatient.

Anger brimmed beneath the surface.

If the hollow clang mocked him one more time, he would throw his damn boot at it.

Where the hell had she got to?

This was the reason he preferred to be alone: the endless worry, the vivid images painting one distressing picture after another. He hated the thinking, the guessing, the waiting—the fear that gripped his heart with its sharp talons and refused to let go.

"That's it," he shouted to no one other than himself. What was he supposed to do, sit there until midnight? He would be fit for Bedlam if he waited a moment longer. The sound of ticking clocks haunting him in his dreams, the repetitive ringing like a death knell.

Jumping to his feet, he made for the door and decided to peruse the displays, to hound Mr. Pearce, to rip the place apart if only to satisfy the torment raging within. Then he heard the echo of footsteps moving along the hallway, the light, yet purposeful strides no doubt belonging to the lady in question.

With a disgruntled huff, he yanked open the door to find her happy countenance peering over a mound of parcels as she smiled back at him.

"Mr. Stone," she said with some surprise as the packages wobbled in her arms. "I was not expecting to see you today."

Not expecting to see him?

Not expecting to see him!

Mere hours ago she had fled his house in a state of terror. She had sought comfort in his arms, lay naked in his bed, run home with her emotions in tatters. What the hell was she expecting?

"Where have you been?" The words came out exactly as he intended: dark, menacing and resentful. They were the words of a cuckold, of a jealous lover, of an overbearing parent.

She ignored the question completely. "Well, are you going to help me with my parcels or are you going to stand there like a bear forced from hibernation?"

With a huff and a noise resembling a growl, he scooped the parcels from her arms and plonked them on the desk.

"Be careful with those," she said, and then her face lit up into one of her illuminating smiles. "Wait until I show you what I've bought." The smile turned coy, sultry. "I think you will like them all."

His head threatened to explode with anger, his body threatened to explode with lust. If he carried on like this, he would be the first person ever to volunteer for Bedlam.

"I have been waiting for hours. I had no idea what had happened to you."

She stopped abruptly and stared at him. Closing the gap between them, she placed a gloved hand on his cheek, traced the line of his jaw. "I did not know you were here, Gabriel."

Damn.

Her sensual tone managed to penetrate his ire, and so he did the only thing he knew would placate his pounding head and racing heart. He drew her into an embrace and devoured her mouth until she gasped and moaned in his arms. Leaning back against the desk, he pulled her between his legs, letting her feel the evidence of his passion, his pain.

Heavens above, he would take her right now if he could. He would take her right there on the desk, her naked body writhing amongst the parcels, papers and ink while his loud roar of satisfaction rumbled through the museum.

Then the blasted clock chimed six.

Gabriel tore his lips from hers, his irate gaze boring holes into the long-case clock behind her.

"I think I will take the key to that thing and throw it in the Thames," he said.

Rebecca considered his mood, which despite the noisy clock, was calmer than when she first arrived. "It is not as loud as some I have heard."

"Trust me. It is loud enough." With a deep sigh, he turned his attention to her. "You seem happier than you did this morning. I had visions of finding you weeping inconsolably as I know how much the painting means to you. I know how I would feel given the circumstances."

It's the same with Mr. Stone ... he needs you, miss.

Higson's words drifted through her mind.

Wedged between Gabriel's muscular thighs, she placed her hand on his chest and felt the wild beat of his heart pulsating beneath her fingers. "I thought so, too, but your man Higson is very wise. He made me see that the important memories are locked away safely in my mind. The painting is just an object and can be repaired or replaced."

"Higson?" he asked, his brow raised in a look of utter disbelief. "Higson offered council in matters of the heart?

Higson talked about his emotions?"

Rebecca nodded, feeling somewhat privileged to have been party to such an enlightening conversation. "He did. I have never met anyone so perceptive. Well, at least not a coachman."

"Could the day possibly be more surprising?"

She stepped out from between his legs and rifled through the packages. "I think I can answer that. There are three more surprises here. This one is for you," she said, handing him a rectangular one. "It is just a little something."

Gabriel turned it over in his hand. "What is it?"

"You will need to open it to find out." She watched him untie the string.

When his hesitant fingers pulled off the paper, a tickling sensation formed in her stomach. With excited curiosity, he turned the leather-bound book over to examine the writing on the spine before meeting her gaze with a look that was difficult to define.

He swallowed visibly. "I do not know what to say."

"Please tell me it is not one you have already?"

"No," he whispered.

"There are only three chapters covering Egypt, I know, but the plate engravings are truly remarkable, particularly the ones of Alexandria and Aswan." She leant across him and flicked to the relevant page. "See."

When she looked up at him, he was not looking at the engraving; he was looking at her with a level of intensity that warmed her to her core.

"I … I am speechless."

Rebecca smiled. "Don't worry. When you see the next item, you truly will be lost for words."

Well, probably not lost for words, she thought, probably so angry he would struggle to get the words out. She hoped the third item would also render him speechless but for an entirely different reason.

The second parcel was square and much larger than the first, deeper, too. Under his watchful gaze, Rebecca opened it to reveal an oak box.

"Can you guess what it is?" she asked, enjoying herself immensely.

Gabriel glanced down at the inlaid box, his brows drawn together. His face grew solemn as he mouthed the words *John Brown* and *London*. "I hope it's not what I think it is."

Rebecca flicked the brass catch and opened the lid to reveal the plush burgundy lining. "Only the finest pair of over and under flintlock pistols you will ever see," she said, running her fingers over the cold metal stock in admiration. "They're made small enough to fit into a pocket or a reticule. What do you think?"

Gabriel's mouth opened and closed a few times before he finally said, "I think you have lost your mind. Do you even know how to use them?"

"Of course." She chuckled. "Mr. Cutter was very attentive and gave me a thorough demonstration."

"Indeed. I'm sure he did."

"Would you like me to show you?"

"No!" he cried. "Rebecca, please tell me you do not intend to carry one of those things around with you?"

"Of course not," she groaned. "I will keep one under my pillow at night in case of intruders and the other one in the top drawer of this desk."

Gabriel placed his book on the wooden counter and rested the weight of his body on his knuckles. With his head bent low, he whispered, "Heaven help me."

"Surely you did not expect me just to sit here like a pheasant waiting to be plucked. I should think you'd be pleased I can protect myself. You've been neglecting your work, and it is my fault. This way you won't have to worry."

"Lately, all I seem to do is worry," he said, straightening. "Now I can add murder to the list of things to fret over. Without a steady aim, it is impossible to hit the intended target."

Rebecca shrugged as she closed the box and secured the catch. "I doubt I will need to use them. Are you staying for dinner?"

He appeared shocked at her question. "Dinner? Rebecca, after what happened here yesterday, I am staying the night."

The words caused a tightening in her stomach that pulsated all the way down her legs to the tips of her toes. She had been waiting to hear him say those words although she did not intend to make it easy for him.

"There's no need. I will be fine now I have Mr. Brown's wonderful inventions. Besides, I'm sure it must be a terrible inconvenience, having to chaperone me when you could be immersed in your books."

His gaze turned dark, brooding. "You don't want me to stay?"

Inside she was smiling, but she kept her expression indifferent. "Do you want to stay?"

"I do not want to leave you here alone."

Did she need to strap him to the rack and crank the handle to gain a confession? Even then, the sound of crunching bones would still render him mute.

"I have been alone for a very long time," she said. "Another night will not make any difference. If you want to spend time in my company, then by all means, you are welcome to stay. If your reasons stem from a sense of duty or responsibility, then I would prefer you didn't."

He was silent, and she could imagine the battle within—

the questions, the fears, the doubts. If he walked away, then that was the end of it. If he stayed, then it was only the beginning.

"You know the answer, Rebecca."

She raised a challenging brow. "Sadly, I do not have the power to read minds. What if I guessed and got it completely wrong?"

His mouth curved into a mischievous grin, and she breathed a sigh of relief. "Now you're teasing me. You know I want to stay."

Finally! She felt like dropping to her knees and praising the Lord.

"We have a few hours before dinner. If you want to, you could help me in the storeroom. I have been sorting through the boxes, but I shall tell you more about it when we sit down to eat."

"Then lead the way," he said, shrugging out of his coat. He draped it over the chair and then gestured to the remaining package. "What's in the last parcel, a cutlass and a bottle of rum?"

"I'm glad to see you have not lost your wit," she said as she ran her hand over the last box. She gave it an admiring caress, causing a rush of anticipation to thrum through her veins. Tonight, she would make another memory. One never to be erased or eradicated, one she would always treasure. "But I'm afraid you will have to wait until after dinner to find out what's in this box."

CHAPTER 19

"*Y*ou're not still sulking about the pistols?"

"I'm not sulking." Gabriel pushed the large crate against the wall and brushed the dust from his hands. "I'm just wondering why we are sorting the artefacts into two separate piles."

He had spent the last hour rummaging through crates and moving boxes. Now, the room looked neat and orderly while his mind was in complete disarray.

It wasn't anger that troubled him or the frustration of sitting in Rebecca's office thinking all sorts of unimaginable things. It wasn't even the fact that his weak heart had skipped a few beats when presented with the fine pair of pistols. Even so, he would track down Mr. Cutter and advise him against selling weaponry to a woman. It was his reaction to her gift, to the leather-bound book. That was what he kept replaying over in his head.

He'd been given gifts before, always books on Egypt, always books to help with his studies. So why was this one any different? Why did all the muscles and bones in his body feel soft and limp?

In those short hours, while she ran about in a desperate bid to find a way to protect herself, she had stopped and thought about him. The gift was to please him, to make him happy, to show she cared. It had nothing to do with advancing his education and the thought caused his heart to ache with a level of tenderness he had never experienced before.

"It will all become clear," she said, and it took him a moment to realise she had answered the question about the separate piles. Removing two clay figures from a small box, she added, "I think you can put these on your list. The ones I have on display are much finer examples."

"You're being very secretive. It makes me think I should be worried." He dipped the nib into the inkwell that sat on top of one of the crates and scratched a few notes while she repackaged the item.

"There's no need to worry. I'll tell you all about it over dinner when there are no distractions." She pointed to the wall behind him. "Put this box over there to the right, as they are the items on your list. It will be easier now they're all separated."

Gabriel nodded, feeling more like the hired help than an expert in Egyptian antiquities. Indeed, his muscles ached, he was hungry, dirty and his erratic emotions made him feel like a bear with a thorn in his paw.

"Right." With a satisfied smile, she braced her hands on her hips and surveyed their work. "We should wash before dinner, and I will quickly change."

Gabriel brushed his hand down his dusty breeches. "I'm afraid I don't have that luxury, so you will just have to accept me as I am."

She stepped closer, close enough to rest her hand on his chest. "Oh, I wouldn't change you for the world," she said before sweeping out of the room.

Dinner comprised of roast duck with artichokes, the platter large enough to feed four.

"Either Mrs. James knows I'm staying for dinner or she is trying to fatten you up in the hope of dissuading me from ravishing you."

"I think it is a little late for her to worry about my virtue, don't you?" she said from the opposite end of the table.

Gabriel should have felt guilty for robbing her future husband of that pleasure, yet he felt ecstatic. The idea of any other man claiming the right roused murderous thoughts.

"You mean it is a case of closing the stable door after the horse has bolted," he said, using a common analogy.

Rebecca smiled at him. "Well, this horse has no intention of returning to the stable. She has no intention of looking back as she is far happier running freely through the fields."

Her words conjured an image of him laying his fiery-haired beauty down in a lush green meadow, of him riding her until he was free from the past, free from the curse that plagued him. "You make freedom sound so tempting," he said, his tone conveying a seductive lilt.

"Then turn your back on it all and run with me, Gabriel," she said softly, coming round the table to refill his glass.

My God, how he wanted to. If only it were possible. If only he were a different man.

"Let me pour the wine," he said, dragging his thoughts from a dream-like state back to the present.

"You are my guest, and I am here to serve."

He watched her glide back to her seat before taking a large mouthful of claret. She shook visibly from the potency of the alcohol, and it occurred to him she was using it for courage.

"Are you going to tell me why we've made two lists? Why the storeroom contains two separate stacks of boxes and crates?" he said, guessing this was the reason she gulped her wine.

Her eyes widened. "Oh, yes. Well, other than the last parcel, I do have another surprise."

"Will I need a large shot of brandy?"

She bit down on her lip like a naughty little imp. "That might be a good idea."

He muttered a curse. "Rebecca, it was a joke. Please tell me I'm not going to have something else to worry about?"

"No, not at all." She shook her head. "I rather hope you will be excited. You see, I have decided to sell all the items on your list. They are surplus to requirements and I need the money."

Gabriel sat up in the chair. "Sell them? Rebecca, if you need money, then I am more than happy to help. You do not need to sell the things most precious to you."

"Don't you see," she said, her face revealing her excitement. "They are objects, Gabriel, objects I do not need, as there is something far more interesting I can do with the money."

Gabriel frowned, fearing he was not going to like this interesting idea. "So you do not need money to cover household expenses?"

"No," she said, clutching her hands to her chest. "I need the money because I am going to Egypt."

"Egypt!" he cried, shooting out of the chair. The whole world seemed to tilt and sway, and he was in danger of falling into a black hole of oblivion. "Egypt?"

"Yes." She nodded. "I know you're surprised, but is it not a wonderful idea? I think my father would have approved."

"Your father would have taken you over his knee and tanned your backside," he barked, before flopping back into his chair. He wanted his words to offend, to knock sense into that carefree head of hers, to make her understand how ridiculous it sounded.

But the words rebounded off this new, confident cloak she wore. "You know you are far too stuffy. Where is your sense of adventure? What is the point of spending years studying relics when there are hundreds of items buried beneath the sand?"

"Egypt?"

"Oh, Gabriel. Think how amazing it will be to tread in the footsteps of the pharaohs, to see Cairo, Luxor and Alexandria."

Gabriel swallowed down the lump in his throat. His stomach formed intricate knots. His mind bombarded him with questions. How could she think of going out there on her own? What would happen to him if she left? Why did the idea sound so wonderful, yet so damn terrifying at the same time?

"Have you considered the fact it might be dangerous? An unmarried lady living on her own in a foreign land is unheard of," he said, pleased he had spoken calmly as he wanted to scream and shout.

"Gabriel, last night those men could have murdered me in my bed. Indeed, it has made me see that nowhere is truly safe. I can sit here and mourn for a life lost to me, or I can head out into the world and make a new one."

Her words made him question the philosophy he used to justify his seclusion: the justification that it was right to mourn the past as a reminder not to make the same mistakes in the future.

"And as for being unmarried," she continued, "I will tell everyone I am a widow. People are inclined to believe what they hear if the story is told with conviction. You know if I were married, no man would permit such a thing."

"Well, in that we agree."

She took another few sips of claret. "If I ever marry, then I want my sons to be explorers and adventurers. I want my daughters to fight for their right to do the same, to be strong with unshakable resolve."

"Just like their mother," he whispered as the image of two daughters with copper curls and two sons with hair as black as his own danced before his eyes.

"I would not want them to sit around living in the past, Gabriel, and I'm sure my parents didn't want that for me."

He picked his glass up from the table and slouched back in the chair. "Remind me to give Higson his notice when I return or at least nail his tongue to the pillory."

"Higson's words have saved me from a life dominated by grief. Now, I have decided to choose the good memories, to remember my parents are with me always."

"I understand that, Rebecca, but Egypt." He did not want to understand anything that would take her so far away from him. Then it occurred to him that it would take weeks or maybe months to plan for such a trip. He had plenty of time to change her mind. In the meantime, he would go along with her plan. "Then let me buy the items," he said. "I have seen them and know their worth. Let me give you the money to go to Egypt."

"No," she said abruptly.

"No? You would rather see them in the hands of a stranger?"

When she looked at him, her eyes brimmed with compassion. "Gabriel, I would rather throw them in a furnace than have you spend another day locked away in your cellar, studying old relics and whatever else you do there."

His cellar?

Why had she said that? He had not mentioned it before.

The blood drained from his face. His erratic heartbeat pounded in his ears. What the hell had Higson told her? He would nail more than the man's tongue to the pillory.

You have to tell her now.

The words were barely audible beneath the din but grew louder demanding to be heard. All he had to do was open his mouth; all he had to do was trust her with his most precious work.

"I do not study relics in my cellar," he said, his tongue thick as he formed the words.

"I know," she said, and his heart shot up into his mouth. "It's just a figure of speech. I imagine your study has the best light."

Gabriel shook his head. Now that he had found the courage to start, he had to finish. "I do not study relics," he repeated, "because I conduct ... experiments in my cellar."

Her hand dropped from her mouth forcing her to place her glass back on the table. "Experiments? You mean with substances, like an apothecary?"

"No, not like an apothecary."

"Experiments on what then?"

"On organs," he said, feeling beads of perspiration form on his brow.

"Organs!" She jerked her head back from the shock, her eyes wide with alarm and he had no choice now but to try to make her understand. "Please tell me you don't mean human organs."

"No. Not human, but the closest thing—pig organs."

The truth seemed to startle her, and she stared at him, her nose scrunched and wrinkled. "For what purpose?"

Fear choked him as it wrapped its spindly vines around his neck. What if she didn't understand? When he told her, would she look at him differently? Would she struggle to find him desirable; would she see a man who had lost his grip on reality?

Half of him felt relieved, glad she knew the depth of his obsession, even though he had so much more to tell. Half of him wanted to smack his head on the table until he was incapable of thinking anymore.

"Whatever it is, you can tell me," she said, as though she understood the torment raging inside him. "You can trust me, Gabriel."

"You will think me a fool," he said, downing what was left of his wine. "But you must understand, I was still a boy when my mother died." His thoughts drifted back to a time of pain and sadness. "Everything changed after that. I felt alone, isolated, and I clung to her memory because it was all I had. My mother used to tell me stories of Egypt, of the *Arabian Nights* and the *Tale of Nur Al-din Al.* I remember the sultan crossing from Cairo to Jizah on his way to the Pyramids and wished I was riding with him."

Now he had started, the words flowed freely.

Rebecca did not interrupt or question him, but sat and listened.

"I read everything I could about the wonders of ancient Egypt. Years later, I met your father. His lectures were inspiring. He was a man I admired, the sort of man I wanted to become. He made me question the need for preserving the dead, helped me examine ways of preserving the organs without removing them. The mummification process was a way of leaving something solid, something tangible that did not crumble away to dust." Gabriel shook his head and laughed. It sounded ridiculous, even to him. "I can't believe I'm going to say this … but I thought of my mother. If only I had a body preserved in a tomb, then perhaps the hole in my chest would become smaller somehow." He stopped and thrust his hand through his hair. "It is the logic of a madman, I know."

"It is the logic of a man whose heart is filled with sorrow," she whispered.

His head shot up, that one sweet sentence making him feel normal, making him believe his obsession was a natural conclusion drawn from years of suffering. "The strange thing is, I can't stop searching for the answer, even though I still do not really understand the question."

Rebecca smiled. "You do not have to search anymore, Gabriel," she said, "because I understand the question. I know the answer you seek."

CHAPTER 20

It took every ounce of strength Rebecca had to stop the tears from falling. Gabriel looked so tortured, so heartbroken; her heart was bleeding, too.

She understood grief, and now she understood love because she would give everything she had to ease his torment, to lessen the burden he had carried around all these years.

The room fell silent, except for the sound of his ragged breathing, and she pushed herself out of the chair and walked around to kneel at his side.

"Now I know why God saw fit to bring us together," she said, stroking his arm. "Why I seem to understand what you've been searching for."

He dragged his hand down his face, the strain of suppressed emotion evident. "How can you know what drives me when I don't even know myself?"

"Because I know what grief is, Gabriel. I know what it is to want to turn back the clock and make everything right again. I know how it spins us into its web until there is no life beyond, so we are stuck, clinging to the silken thread hoping we can survive a bit longer. I know all we can do is search for the answer to the question: What can I do to live a day without the pain of grief?"

He looked up at her, his weary eyes growing bright with wonder, as though he had crossed oceans and continents on a fool's crusade and had finally stumbled upon a wise mystic with the power to banish ghosts.

"If that is the question," he whispered, "then what is the answer?"

Rebecca put her hand on his cheek. "I shall tell you the answer, Gabriel, but not now. You must be patient. There is something I need to do. Will you wait here while I go and get the parcel?"

"The parcel?" he said, a little confused. "I'd forgotten all about it."

She had distracted his mind, his gaze returning to the present, dragging him back from the dreamy place, exactly as she'd intended.

With Gabriel, there was always an inner struggle. And she could sense these opposed feelings now: relief because they had changed the subject and an impatience to know the answer that had plagued him for so long.

"Perhaps it could wait until tomorrow," he said, his impatience winning the battle.

"It cannot wait." She moved to the table, pulled the crystal top from the decanter and refilled both glasses. With her glass in hand, she walked over to the door. "Give me a moment, and I shall be right back."

Rebecca returned to her chamber, leaving Gabriel to sit alone with his thoughts. Sorrow had kept the excitement at bay and the shock of knowing he had struggled all these years on his own.

Her mind conjured an image of a room filled with glass

jars, of organs bobbing about in a strange brown liquid. She wondered what sad thoughts drifted through his mind when he looked at them.

Organs!

In all her wild imaginings, she would never have guessed that. The fear and apprehension in his eyes made her heart ache. Perhaps he expected her to find the notion weird, to find him abhorrent. But his declaration had made her want to scurry across the table and jump into his arms, to kiss him, declare undying love and ease his torment.

Even now, she hoped she was strong enough to bring her plan to fruition. Gabriel needed her tonight, and she would not disappoint.

Lifting the lid from the box, she stared at the emerald-green gown and put her hand up through the diaphanous material. Without the modesty of a chemise and petticoat, it was completely transparent.

Her mother had worn it respectably. Thanks to Madame Coulter, the hole was unnoticeable, and Rebecca would wear it on its own. Sinfully. Her naked body visible and draped in an emerald shimmer.

In a quick flurry of activity, she undressed. Her hands trembled as she let the material glide down over her bare skin. Despite drinking more claret than usual, she swallowed what remained in the glass and let the warmth infuse her body as she pulled the remaining pins from her hair.

Nerves held her at the chamber door.

What was she thinking?

She was a novice, unskilled in seduction. How would she know what to do? Then she thought that perhaps it wouldn't be too difficult, not if she followed her heart, not if she let desire work its magic.

With that in mind, she crept along the corridor and lingered in the doorway.

Gabriel was still sitting in the chair, cradling his glass, his head bent low as he examined the blood-red liquid. He swished it around and watched it settle.

Sucking in a breath, she tiptoed into the room. "In my excitement, I couldn't help but try it on."

She had to purse her lips when he glanced up. His eyes grew wide and raced over every inch of her body. She noticed him swallow and watched his mouth open and close as he struggled to speak.

"I … I see you saved the best until last," he finally said, moistening his lips.

"Do you like it?" she asked, her tone husky as his gaze fell to her breasts, to the perky nipples that were so pleased he approved.

"To say I like it would be an understatement. This is by far the best surprise of the day."

"Come," she said, taking him by the hands and pulling him to his feet.

He drew her into an embrace, his fingers skimming the curve of her hip, causing the sheer material to tickle and tease her sensitive body.

"No," she whispered as he lowered his head to claim her mouth, "not yet. Tonight we will do things a little differently."

He raised a mischievous brow. A look of intrigue flashed in his eyes, banishing the pain and sorrow. "That sounds interesting."

A pang of doubt flared, and she tried her best to ignore it. "I can promise you it will be," she said, taking his hand and leading him down the dimly lit corridor, aware that the view from behind was utterly scandalous.

She led him into her chamber, stopping to lock the door before pulling him closer to the bed.

"Now I'm your prisoner, what do you intend to do with me?" The tone of his voice suggested he was as eager as she to play these games, and Rebecca wanted nothing more than to please him.

"Don't worry," she said, "nothing torturous, but I will decide what happens. I will seduce you, and you will stand there and let me." Her voice sounded confident now, like the voice of a seasoned courtesan.

Gabriel's ravenous gaze fell to her breasts. "Madam, consider me seduced." He gave a low bow. "But I am forever your humble servant. You may do with me what you will."

Desire burst forth in giant waves, crashing through her body, almost sweeping her off her feet. She had brought him this far, all she needed to do was focus. Think. No, not think, feel. What did she want to do to him? What would he like her to do?

Feeling wickedly sinful, she ran her hands down the front of the thin material, a gentle caress that fluttered over her hips, over the soft curve of her stomach. "I suppose I should wear a chemise under this," she said as her hand crept higher, "and stays to give me some lift just here."

Gabriel sucked in a breath. "I find I like it just the way it is."

"You do? Then perhaps I could wear it to my next ball."

"You'll only ever wear it in my bed," he said, devouring her with his heated gaze.

Rebecca loved seeing him like this, so devilishly handsome, so carefree, so aroused. "I'm going to touch you, Gabriel, but you must promise not to touch me until I allow it. Can you make such a promise?"

The corners of his mouth turned up. "Oh, I promise. I promise to do whatever I'm told."

"Good," she said with some authority. "Take off your boots."

He obliged, and she came to stand in front of him. Her fingers crept up the front of his waistcoat, and she undid the buttons. Pushing it back off his shoulders, she moved to work on his cravat while he simply stood and watched.

She yanked his shirt from his breeches, ran her hands up over the hard planes, the heat from his skin scorching her palms. Standing on her tiptoes, she lifted his shirt up over his head and pressed her body into his; rubbing gently against his bare chest as ripples of pleasure pulsed through her.

Gabriel was true to his word and didn't touch her, but she heard the growl in the back of his throat, watched him lower his head and inhale the scent of her hair.

The sight of him stole her breath: his broad, muscular shoulders, the dusting of dark hair on his chest, the perfectly formed muscles in his abdomen. It took every effort not to jump on him, ravage him, sate her desire and consummate her love. Instead, she circled him slowly, placing kisses on his upper arm and across his back, as her fingers trailed a seductive line in hot pursuit.

"Gabriel," she whispered, coming round to kiss the small dark nipple, flicking her tongue over the peak when he sucked in a breath. "You have the body of a Greek god." She moved to the other side, gathering the courage to bite, nip and lick the bronzed skin that tasted so divine.

The passion burning inside drove her forward. And so she stood on her toes and brushed her lips against his, her fingers following the trail of dark hair down to the band of his breeches. His breathing grew ragged, her head dizzy from the wine, from the feeling of euphoria and she let her hand wander lower down to the fall of his breeches, rubbing against the evidence of his arousal.

"Holy hell," he muttered, closing his eyes. "Tell me I can touch you."

Rebecca smiled. "Not yet," she said softly, and she ran her tongue over his lips, penetrating the moist line until she was inside his mouth. As her hand stroked him, she continued to explore, her tongue tempting, teasing, eliciting a response only to pull away.

"When I said you would be the death of me, I was damn well right. How much longer?"

Rebecca liked this game; she liked having him at her mercy. She liked seeing the pleasure on his handsome face. "Remove your breeches," she demanded. "I want you naked."

He cursed as he stripped off every stitch and then stood before her, hard and glorious.

Her mind raced back to the erotic images stored in the crate, to the ancient Egyptian papyrus she'd found rather enlightening. And with that in mind, she pushed him back until he fell onto the bed.

Gathering up the diaphanous material, she pulled it up over her head. Her body was ready for him, aroused beyond anything she had felt before, and she climbed over him to straddle his hips.

His eyes widened as she took him in hand and directed him to the place that throbbed and ached for his touch. "Not yet," she whispered, determined she would do the claiming, and his hands fell obediently, balling the counterpane into his fists as she lowered herself down slowly.

"Oh, God." He closed his eyes and gave a pleasurable hum when she took the whole length of him.

She could have stayed like that forever, feeling full,

feeling happy. But the desire in her belly compelled her to move even though she wasn't sure how.

Guessing that the principle was the same regardless of the position, she lifted herself up and then sank back down. She knew she had done something right as he muttered a sweet curse and whispered, "Do it again."

As she found a rhythm, he folded his arms behind his head and watched each delicious slide. It was shocking, sinful, so wonderful that she quickened the pace. Feeling the coil inside tighten, her movements grew wild and frantic.

"Now," she breathed, already halfway to heaven.

With a growl, he sat up, grabbed her round the waist and held her tightly against him as he flipped her onto her back. His movements were just as frantic, thrusting hard and deep as she wrapped her legs around him and clawed at his shoulders. She threw her hands behind her head and let him take her; let him ride her until she felt as though she was flying. His hands grasped hers, and he held them there, palm to palm, their fingers clasped, the bed banging against the wall as they found their glorious release together.

CHAPTER 21

*R*ebecca woke to the sound of Gabriel's deep, rhythmical breathing and cuddled into the warm hard body beside her, desperate to keep last night's dream alive.

The night had been spectacular.

He was magnificent.

Just when she thought she couldn't possibly love him more, he did something or said something to make her heart swell. She longed to tell him, and almost blurted it out during the throes of passion, when her mind and body shook with a need only he could sate. When she knew there would never be another, only him.

Feeling desire spark again and remembering how glorious it felt to join with him, she glanced up at his closed lids before peering under the sheet to study the masculine form she found so intriguing.

He felt like marble encased in soft silk. His body had a potent scent, an addictive essence that made her want to rain kisses along his torso, taste the skin stretched taut across his abdomen, to delve lower as she wondered what it would be like to take him in her mouth, to have the power to—

"Did you find what you were looking for?"

His languid voice startled her, and she felt her cheeks flame.

"Yes. I mean no. It's the spider," she said, lifting her head and finding the courage to look at him. "I thought I felt it crawling up my leg and panicked, thinking it had found a way in."

"The spider," he repeated, his eyes alight with amusement. "Then let me offer my assistance."

Without further comment, he dived under the sheet until his head was at her toes. "Did it do this?" he asked, and she felt a light tickling starting at her ankle and running up to the top of her thigh. "Or was it this?"

"Gabriel," Rebecca squealed from the shock, from the excitement, from the pleasure of having him touch her again.

He settled between her legs as his head popped out from under the sheet. "I can't find the spider," he said, rubbing against her in such an intimate way she almost swooned. "But I think I know of a way to distract your mind."

Without another word, he claimed her mouth; moments later he reclaimed her body and let her relive last night's erotic dream.

An hour later, she sat on the stool in front of the mirror trying to style her hair. But the sight of Gabriel's firm buttocks, as he climbed out of bed, proved to be too much of a distraction.

"What are your plans for today?" she asked, believing the conversation would occupy his mind enough to make his movements slow, less hurried.

"I shall return to Hanover Square," he said, dragging up his breeches, and she felt a pang of disappointment. "I need to wash, dress and collect a few things if I'm to stay with you again tonight."

The word *tonight* held a wealth of promise, and she had to curb her excitement. "I have a few things to do, but I shall be perfectly safe during the day. Perhaps if you came back sometime after six," she said, not wanting to rouse his suspicion and knowing it would give her enough time to accomplish her task.

He turned and regarded her with a solemn expression that was so unlike the man who had ravished her in her bed. "On the subject of safety, have you considered the possibility it was not one of the Wellfords who destroyed your mother's portrait?"

"It is not destroyed, Gabriel, just a little damaged, that's all," she said with a weak smile. "Besides, I've not thought of anything as my mind has been somewhat distracted."

He did not look the least bit guilty and instead raised an arrogant brow. "I'd get used to it, as I'm sure you'll be suffering from a similar predicament later this evening."

Good, she thought as desire unfurled in her belly. She wanted him to push the past from his mind. She wanted him to focus on the future.

"If we stand any chance of moving beyond the door of this chamber today, I suggest we change the subject. In answer to your earlier question, I am confident George did not damage the painting. As for the other two, I have no idea what they are capable of."

He pulled his shirt over his head and a tiny groan escaped from her lips.

"Well, it was not Alexander, either," he said.

"How do you know?"

Gabriel paused. "I believe he's away in Italy, probably

painting angels and cherubs and frittering away his inheritance."

Rebecca raised her chin. "Oh, I see. Well, that only leaves Freddie. Now I think about it, the men in the museum had been drinking. And I do remember Freddie being rather inebriated at the Cheltons' ball. Perhaps it was simply a drunken prank. Perhaps his accomplice didn't know the sentimental value of the portrait."

Judging by the look on Gabriel's face, he did not believe that any more than she did, which reminded her she really should try loading the pistol.

"What about the gentlemen at the ball, the ones you refused to dance with? Did you get the sense they felt slighted in any way?"

She shook her head, dismissing the shiver running up her spine as she remembered the lecherous looks. "No, not at all."

"What of the gentleman I almost murdered on the terrace?"

"He was simply looking for easy entertainment." She caught his troubled gaze in the mirror, saw the cogs turning and wondered what he was thinking.

"You're probably right," he said. "I'll wager Freddie had something to do with it. No doubt guilt will plague him until he feels forced to confess."

"I'm certain of it," she lied. The look of panic in his eyes was unmistakable. She would do more than try to load her pistol; she would carry it with her wherever she went.

Gabriel strode over to her and placed a chaste kiss to her temple. "I shall return at six. Will you have any more surprises for me?"

Only one, she thought, knowing he was not going to like it. "You mean you're hoping I will seduce you again."

Gabriel laughed, although it failed to reach his eyes. "Hoping, no. Praying, yes."

"Then I shall rummage through the crate of erotic etchings in the hope of finding inspiration," she said with a coy smile.

As she watched him walk out of the door, she hoped he would still desire her when she told him what she had done, or more precisely, where she had been.

Rebecca took a hackney to Bedford Square, relieved to find George Wellford at home and, after a brief absence, Winters returned to escort her into the study.

George stood to greet her but did not walk around the desk. "Rebecca. What a pleasant surprise." He looked beyond her shoulder. "Are you alone?"

It was an odd question. No doubt he assumed Gabriel accompanied her everywhere. "Of course," she said, glancing at the oak cabinets lined with books and imagining her father rifling through them. "Who else were you expecting?"

"No one." George shook his head numerous times and gestured to the chair opposite his desk. "Only, the last few times we've met, Mr. Stone is often trailing behind, barking and snapping at your heels like an annoying little terrier."

Rebecca pulled off her gloves, sat down and feeling rather defensive said, "Mr. Stone has been extremely kind and considerate to me, my lord. *Annoying* is certainly not a word I would use to describe him." Indeed, the words *handsome and sinful with a wicked tongue* sprang to mind.

"You're right," George replied with a dismissive wave, "it was not a very good description. Perhaps a frustrated little terrier is more accurate."

Rebecca looked down her nose at him and huffed. "I did not come here to discuss the character traits of dogs. But I did come here to talk to you about Mr. Stone."

George sat up in his chair. "Has he declared his intentions?"

"Of course not."

He looked disappointed. "Would you like him to?"

"No!" she said, lying for the second time in one day. "Perhaps you should stop asking questions and listen. You sound like an old matron desperate to hear the latest gossip." He accepted her criticism and conceded by gesturing for her to continue. "I was wondering if you knew where I could find Mr. Stone's sister and her mother. I'm assuming they live in London and thought I would pay them a visit."

"Does Mr. Stone know you intend to call upon them?"

"You've asked another question, George. And no, he does not know I intend to call on them else I would have asked him for their address."

George opened his mouth, but promptly closed it again and then spent a moment examining her face. "When you talk about Mr. Stone you have a certain twinkle in your eye, a certain look that makes me wonder if the term *friend* is the appropriate word to define your relationship."

Rebecca blinked but could not stop the heat rising to her cheeks. If George could read that in her eyes, what else was she giving away? Did he know she was in love with Gabriel, that he made her body tremble simply by speaking her name?

"Mr. Stone is my dearest friend, the only person I can trust. I would expect my eyes to twinkle with respect when mentioning the name of the man who has done his utmost to help me."

The corners of George's mouth twitched, but he did not smile. "I trust he is proving to be satisfactory?"

Rebecca almost choked on the lump that formed in her throat. "I don't know what you mean."

"As your chaperone. I trust he is proving to be a reliable companion," he clarified. "I hope you know I had nothing to do with what happened at the museum this time. I would never damage something so precious out of spite or jealousy."

Had Gabriel told him about her mother's painting?

Her thoughts drifted back to the conversation in her office, where Gabriel had told her he wanted to stay and implied it had nothing to do with duty or responsibility. She could not help but think it was a lie.

"Mr. Stone came to see you?" she asked, her vision blurring. "He told you about the painting? He told you he would act as a chaperone?"

"I believe he thought we were responsible for damaging the painting and sought vengeance for the distress caused. Freddie has been avoiding me, but I am to meet with him later, although I doubt him capable of making it up your stairs let alone anything else." He sighed, and his gaze softened. "I understand why you feel you cannot trust me. I had to trust Stone. He is the only person who is close to you and one has to admire his commitment to your cause."

Commitment!

Had Gabriel stayed the night purely out of a sense of obligation?

"I thought you said his morbid fascination with the dead was no good for me," she challenged, conjuring an image of an underground vault and her wounded heart trapped in a jar, withering before her eyes.

George shrugged. "I wanted to make him angry. I wanted him to rescue you from the Egyptian tomb you call a home. I wanted him to prove me wrong."

Oh, Gabriel had certainly proved him wrong.

"Well, where has your meddling got you, my lord? I have just sat here and told you he is the only person I trust and yet you had to find a way of ruining it. I asked Gabriel not to tell you about the painting or the intruders," she said, aware she had spoken his name so intimately and without thought. "With your flippant remarks, you have shown him to be untrustworthy. You have managed to destroy the only thing that means anything to me. So ask yourself this, why would I ever trust you when you seek to hurt me at every opportunity?"

Rebecca stood and thrust her gloves on so fiercely she was in danger of fracturing a finger. "Stay away from me and stop interfering in my life," she barked as she turned towards the door.

"Rebecca," he called after her, a hint of desperation in his voice. "Sometimes arrogance gets the better of me. Sometimes, in a bid to prove my worth, I go about things the wrong way." Her father's blue eyes looked up at her, all sad and forlorn. "A week ago I would not have been able to help you. But since learning of your friendship with Mr. Stone, well—you will find his sister, Ariana, on George Street, number thirty-six."

CHAPTER 22

*N*umber thirty-six, a mid-terrace house of excellent proportions, looked clean and well maintained. While Gabriel failed to provide emotional support, he obviously had no problem when it came to his financial responsibilities.

"Do you want me to wait?" the hackney driver called out to her. "It's four and six every half hour."

Rebecca raised a brow at the extortionate price, the man shrugging in response as he flashed a mouth full of rotten teeth. "No, I don't need you to wait," she said, thrusting the two-shilling fare into his greedy palm. Besides, the walk home would give her an opportunity to think and prepare for the blazing row she knew would follow.

She had just as much right to be angry.

Against her wishes, Gabriel had colluded with George Wellford. He'd plotted and schemed as though caring for a child in need of coddling. It took every effort to suppress the feeling of betrayal, a feeling that threatened to poison her heart and contaminate her thoughts.

But if she stepped inside his sister's house, was she not just as guilty of deceit?

With a deep sigh, she turned to face the facade and spotted someone watching her from an upstairs window. The young girl was petite and delicate of frame with hair as black as coal.

The scene reminded her of the first time she'd seen Gabriel's handsome face peering out of his front window. She had thought him cold, heartless and downright rude. In stark contrast, this girl held up a dainty hand and waved, leaving Rebecca no choice but to wave back, no choice now but to knock.

A woman no older than twenty opened the door. Her warm smile was enhanced by hair the shade of wheat on a summer's day. The loose strands poking out of the mobcap gave the impression she'd pulled it on in a hurry and wasn't used to answering the door.

"Can I help you?"

"My name is Miss Linwood. I am acquainted with Mr. Gabriel Stone. He has asked me to call in and pay my respects to his family." Rebecca would have to perform some sort of penance for the lies she had told today.

Lately, she seemed to have a weakness for all things sinful.

"Mr. Stone asked you to call?" the woman said with a shocked expression as though the man they were discussing had been dead for years and must have called out to her from the grave.

"He asked me to send his regards to Ariana and Mrs. Stone," Rebecca said, feeling the need to justify the reason for her visit to a maid. After all, there was always a chance she would close the door in her face.

The woman examined Rebecca's attire and, after giving a

satisfactory nod, welcomed her into the hallway. "Please wait here while I go fetch the mistress," she said, bobbing a half curtsy.

As Rebecca stared at the tasteful décor, the girl from the upstairs window appeared on the top stair. Her gaze was cautious in assessment as one would expect from a child in the presence of a stranger. Curiosity got the better of her, and she took a hesitant step, her knuckles white where she gripped the handrail for support.

"You must be Ariana," Rebecca said, offering a kind smile. "I can see you have inherited your brother's dark hair."

Ariana's eyes widened, and she took another step. "Do you know my brother?" she asked, the admiration in her voice reflected in her eyes.

"Yes, I know him very well. Who do you think sent me here today?"

Guilt flared as she remembered Gabriel's words. He considered them estranged, and so kept his distance. The child's mother could have told a tale to account for his absence, and Rebecca felt foolish for speaking without thought.

Ariana smiled. "Mama said I will see him again soon when he is not so busy with his studies. Did he send you here all the way from Egypt?"

Rebecca thought her heart might break and shatter into a thousand tiny pieces. "No, I have not come from Egypt. But your brother wrote and asked me to call."

The sound of footsteps hurrying along the hallway caught Rebecca's attention. She looked up to see the lady of the house, her auburn hair tied in a simple knot that softened her features. Her yellow gown was plain and unadorned. Rebecca got the impression she was a woman unimpressed with frivolities.

"Ariana, I thought you were upstairs," the lady said, her blue eyes flashing with mild panic.

"Forgive me" Rebecca inclined her head. "I'm afraid I encouraged her to come down. My name is Rebecca Linwood. I own an Egyptian museum in Coventry Street."

"I knew you'd come from Egypt," Ariana said with a little giggle.

"I am Sarah Stone. Won't you join us for tea?"

Ariana rushed to the bottom stair. "Oh, do say you'll stay," she blurted. "You can tell me all about the Pyramids and—"

"Ariana," her mother berated. "We do not pester our guests."

"Thank you, Mrs. Stone," Rebecca said, giving the child a sly wink. "I would love to take tea with you."

Sarah Stone sent her daughter to the kitchen to keep the maid company while she waited for the tea tray, on the understanding she could join them a little later.

"I can take your bonnet," Mrs. Stone said, escorting Rebecca into the drawing room. "I only keep a small staff as it suits our needs," she added by way of explanation and gestured to the gold damask chairs. "Thank you for not telling Ariana that her brother lives ten minutes away."

Rebecca handed her bonnet to Mrs. Stone, who placed it on the sideboard. "I can see she admires him a great deal," she said, patting down the stray curls as she took a seat.

Sarah Stone sat opposite. "Ariana hasn't seen Gabriel since their father died. She thinks he is away in Egypt, digging in the sand and riding camels. She has this fanciful notion that he is princely and important. I do not want to shatter her illusion, not just yet."

The softly spoken words held a hint of bitterness. Rebecca felt torn. Part of her wanted to admonish the man she loved for being neglectful, for being so insular. Indeed, she could have kicked him in the shin for not seeing what a treasure he had for a sister.

But Gabriel was misunderstood. He had let grief rule his heart, and she could not blame him for that.

"I'm sure he doesn't mean to be so detached," Rebecca said, the desire to defend him overriding everything else. "What others regard as unforgivable can often be justified within our own minds."

Sarah Stone held her hands together as though in prayer, the tips of her fingers supporting her chin. "May I ask how you are acquainted with Gabriel?"

They were acquainted in the most intimate way a man and woman could be. "He is a partner in the museum and a very dear friend."

"I see. Have you known him long?"

With her prying questions, Sarah Stone sounded like George. What was she supposed to say? That she had only known him for a week? "We've been friends for a while."

With a curious hum, Sarah brought her fingers to her lips and tapped gently, before smiling like a mother party to her child's secrets. "I know Gabriel didn't ask you to come here. So I wonder why it is you came?"

Because she loved him.

Because she wanted to help him forget the past, to reconnect with his family.

Because she knew what it felt like to be alone and isolated.

"I have always believed my half-brothers despised me and thought me the cause of their anguish," Rebecca said, knowing honesty was the best option. She had told enough lies for one day. "It's a feeling I've come to live with, but I cannot stand back and watch someone else suffer the same injustice. I know Gabriel does not mean to hurt anyone. He has not truly come to terms with his mother's death, and I think it causes him to be distant."

Sarah Stone fell silent for what seemed like an hour, yet it was mere seconds. "I believe Gabriel spent too much time listening to gossip. We were never in love, his father and I," she said, gazing past Rebecca's shoulder. "He was lonely and broken, and I needed his protection. Our partnership served us both well although Gabriel struggled to accept it. I did everything I could to welcome him," she continued, her words genuine and not the least bit defensive. "I knew he found it difficult but almost twelve years have passed. I suppose I thought things would change and he would learn to accept us."

Time did not always heal wounds. Resentment often acted as a mask to hide the pain festering away underneath. "I know from experience that sometimes it's easier to live in the past. The past is familiar. It is where we take comfort. That is why I have come. I want to help him move forward, to have a future, to be happy."

"I believe you have set yourself a mammoth task."

A light tap on the drawing room door interrupted the intimacy of the moment, and the maid entered carrying a tray. Ariana poked her head around the jamb, and her mother gestured for her to enter.

"Do you think Gabriel has found anything exciting on his adventures?" Ariana said, coming to stand next to Rebecca's chair as the maid poured the tea.

Rebecca considered inviting them to the museum but hesitated. "Well, he sent a package of clay figures for me to display in the museum. Perhaps I could bring one for you to look at."

Ariana glanced at her mother. "I have never seen anything from Egypt before. Could Miss Linwood call again, Mama?"

Sarah Stone smiled and nodded. "Miss Linwood is welcome to call again."

They conversed about the weather and Ariana's birthday. The child giggled with excitement even though it was more than a month away. When it was time to leave, Sarah escorted Rebecca to the door.

"If you do decide to tell Gabriel you were here, please tell him I asked after him."

Anxiety flared when Rebecca thought of his reaction, and she pushed it aside. "I shall tell him what an angel Ariana is. I shall tell him we need to make room at the museum for a third partner."

"You're very kind," she replied with a smile. "Does Gabriel know you're in love with him?"

Rebecca froze. Was it so obvious? Had some mischievous imp carved the words into her forehead for all to see?

"Of course not," she said, trying to sound amused. "If he did, I imagine he would be on the first boat to Cairo."

CHAPTER 23

*R*ebecca stepped out onto George Street, instinct dragging her gaze away from the row of houses, telling her to look up at the window.

As suspected, Ariana had rushed upstairs to wave good-bye, her face squashed against the glass as she tried to get Rebecca's attention. Touched that the child held her in such high regard, Rebecca waved back.

Bless her.

Ariana looked a little distraught, a little emotional. But then children were quick to form attachments, and Rebecca got the impression she spent much of her time alone indoors.

Not wanting to distress the child any further, Rebecca looked away and quickened her pace, keen to be out of her line of sight.

Even so, she was in no rush to get home.

After such a pleasant afternoon, the thought of facing Gabriel filled her with dread. She didn't want to rouse his anger. She didn't want to see coldness and disappointment in his eyes, not when—

Feeling a sudden jolt, Rebecca lurched forward, sucking in a breath as someone barged into her from behind. She glanced over her shoulder and saw the outline of a man walking so close his arm brushed against her back.

With the pavement being wide enough for three people, she had a good mind to turn around and chastise him for such disgraceful conduct.

Then she heard his steely voice whisper in her ear, the tone cold and unforgiving as the tip of a sharp object dug into her back. "If you make a sound or glance behind again, I will bury this blade so far into your back you will feel its hilt."

The hairs on her nape prickled to attention. The shiver shooting down her spine made her teeth chatter, and her tongue felt thick as she tried to form a response.

"If it's money you want, th-then take my reticule." She thrust out her arm in the hope of enticing him away.

"I don't want money," he said with a sneer as he slapped her arm down. "You see the carriage up ahead? I want you to open the door and climb inside."

She contemplated making a dash for it, but with a petticoat and gown flapping around her ankles he would soon catch up with her.

Guessing the train of her thoughts, he added, "Don't forget, I know where the little girl lives. It would be a terrible tragedy if something should happen to her."

If Rebecca ever got out of this mess, she would punch him on the nose for that comment.

Coming to an abrupt halt next to the unmarked carriage, she glanced up at the driver hoping to exchange a silent plea. But the scrawny man just stared out into the distance, showing no interest in the criminal activities of his master.

"Get in."

Rebecca hesitated. "Are you going to tell me where we're going?"

He reached around her waist and opened the carriage door. "I said get in."

"Miss Linwood. Miss Linwood."

The words were a distant echo, a cry, an appeal.

Rebecca looked back to see Sarah Stone hurrying down the empty street towards them, waving her hand in the air to draw attention. The man cursed. The long string of obscenities sounded vicious, venomous. He shoved Rebecca into the carriage, climbed in behind her and slammed the door.

Before they'd settled into their seats, the carriage jerked forward, causing them both to stumble. The sound of the knife skittering across the floor captured their attention.

With lightning speed, Rebecca dived down, desperate to be the first to reach the blade. The tips of her fingers grazed against the metal. A mad scramble ensued. Using all of his weight, he knocked her onto her side and crushed her against the seat. When he wrapped his hand around the handle, the rush of disappointment was almost painful.

With a secure grip, he waved the knife at her face, and she scampered back up onto the seat. "Try that again and you'll have an ugly scar, one to remind you of your stupidity."

She imagined the reflection from the sharpened edge, bright and glaring as it sliced through her skin, sawed through her flesh, the scorching pain like nothing she'd ever felt before. When his arm twitched, she winced, but he lowered the knife, and her shoulders sagged as she breathed a sigh.

The threat of violence hung in the air.

He leant forward, picked his hat up off the carriage floor and placed it next to him on the seat. With a clear view of his face, she knew she had seen him before. Familiarity banished some of her fear.

"I believe we've met," she said, remembering the apprehension in his eyes when challenged by Gabriel. It gave her a little more confidence to be brazen. "At the Cheltons', I recall. Were you not of the opinion that those with questionable lineage had questionable morals?"

Surely this act of revenge didn't stem from being passed over in the ballroom. Gabriel's threat to knock his teeth down his throat hardly warranted kidnap and common assault.

He ignored her question. His mouth thinned into a menacing line, the black beads for eyes still hard and unreadable. "Why do you call yourself Linwood when you are obviously a Wellford?"

Rebecca wondered if the words tasted as sour as they sounded. She had a good mind to tell him to go to the devil but knew if she had any hope of escaping, she would need to be co-operative. "There are many reasons. To save my brothers the embarrassment of having a sister who works for a living. To save me the embarrassment of being associated with those who despise me."

"You're lying," he spat. "Is that what you tell yourself when you want sympathy? That everyone despises you? Poor little Rebecca, all lost and alone with no one to love. Is that what you tell your scholar friend?" He shrugged. "Where is he now when you need him most?"

She struggled to follow his meaning. His thoughts lacked unity and flitted back and forth, somewhat fragmented. Was his gripe with her or with Gabriel?

"If you believe I'm lying, why do you think I chose the name Linwood?" Perhaps if she got him to talk for a while, he would reveal his motive for kidnapping her in broad daylight.

He sat forward, his arms resting on his knees. "Because

you refuse to acknowledge your father, you refuse to acknowledge his name. Oh, you're probably not even aware that's the reason, and so you find other ways to explain the shame he brought to your door."

"Shame? I feel no shame. I loved my father. I still love him."

Her words roused his temper, his face flushing red, his teeth grinding together. "Love!" he said with contempt. "Love is a term of endearment, of deep affection. What would your father know of that? Thanks to him your lineage is tainted, your reputation tainted. Everyone who associates with you is tainted."

Did this have something to do with her father, then?

"You knew my father?"

"I hear the surprise in your voice. You ask a question, but you do not want to hear the answer. Yes, I knew your father."

Rebecca stared at him. He was older than her, she guessed around thirty. She stared at his black eyes, black hair and his olive complexion. His face was so opposed to her father's sunny disposition. Surely this man wasn't … surely they were not related. The thought caused a gigantic hole to open up in her stomach.

"Are you … Was my father—"

He snorted. The fake laugh was designed to express his contempt. "I am not your brother if that is what you're thinking. I am not your father's son. I'm some other lord's by-blow."

Relief flashed through her, but it was short lived. What other possible reason could there be for such a display of vehemence?

"What do you want from me?" she asked, dreading the answer. "Where are we going?"

A smile played at the corners of his mouth although his eyes revealed no pleasure. "We are going to a playhouse. We will just be in time for the performance. The rest, well, it will soon become apparent."

CHAPTER 24

Gabriel removed the iron key from the drawer of his desk and rolled it over in his hand. The palm of his empty hand twitched, eager for something heavy: for a mallet or a hammer. He would go down the rickety stairs into his cellar and smash the glass domes, the wooden shelves, the bottles of chemicals, salts and oils.

In a rampant rage, he would grit his teeth, bite down on the inside of his cheek until the taste of warm metal coated his tongue. The drawing of blood would be like a purge, to purify and cleanse away his shame, to rid himself of the burden that consumed him.

Since opening his heart to Rebecca, the house was no longer a sanctuary. It felt like a prison. The key was a gateway to the past, to a cell that would see him rot away in isolation for the next twenty years, if he so wished.

Now, he had found sanctuary in the form of a luscious fiery-haired temptress. In the arms of a woman who made him feel alive and free, deep inside a woman who ignited a fire in his soul as well as in his loins.

"Rebecca."

He said the word aloud. It was a way of expressing his affection, to prove these experiences were real and not a wonderful dream of fulfilled desires, to banish the fear of waking to gut-wrenching disappointment.

The clock on the mantel struck one. One solitary chime to mock him, to taunt him, to remind him he needed to get used to being alone again. If Rebecca got her wish, she would soon be far away, riding through the sandy dunes of Egypt on a wild adventure.

Egypt!

A weird puffing sound escaped from his lips: contempt for her elevated ideas, for making the unrealistic sound possible.

What the hell would she do in Egypt?

The stifling heat crippled the locals. For her, it would be unbearable. The beads of sweat would trickle all the way down the curve of her spine, a cool refreshing bath the only way to ease the discomfort. She'd be forced to abandon all clothing and lie naked in bed. The markets would be filled with exotic fruits that left a mouthful of juice, the taste unusual, sweet and delicious. The music would sound different, not precise or rigid, but more carefree, a sensual blend to stimulate and arouse the senses.

Bloody hell!

He threw the key back in the drawer and with a frustrated sigh pushed his hand through his hair. If the lure of the Orient sounded so tempting to him, what chance did he have of changing Rebecca's mind? Of course, in desperation he could always turn to Lord Wellford, certain he would strictly forbid such a venture.

As though Gabriel had summoned the man purely by thought alone, Cosgrove knocked the door. He held it ajar and blocked the entrance. "Lord Wellford is here, sir. I am afraid he gave me no option but to invite him in."

Gabriel opened his mouth to speak, but the door burst open, hitting the wall with all the force of a hurricane. George Wellford barged past Cosgrove, dragging another man—who Gabriel assumed was Frederick—by the arm.

"Go on, tell him," Wellford said, catapulting Frederick into the middle of the room without a greeting or an apology for the intrusion. "Tell him what you've done."

Frederick lifted his head and threw his hands up in the air. "I do not see what it has to do with him. I do not see why you saw fit to drag me halfway across town on a fool's errand."

"I assume you're talking about the incident at the museum," Gabriel said grimly.

Wellford huffed and shook his head. "It appears Frederick is the one who broke into Rebecca's house. It appears Frederick is a complete idiot."

"You're the idiot," Frederick cried. "You were the one who led her to believe in a curse. You were the one who told me you wanted to prove she was not safe on her own."

"That was for her own good," Wellford said. "I did not damage her most treasured possession in the process."

"Neither did I."

"Enough!" Gabriel yelled. Anger rose up, ready to boil over into something far more damaging.

Rebecca would react badly to the news.

If they were his brothers, he would run as far away as he possibly could. Perhaps that was why Alexander had fled to Italy in the hope of becoming a painter. Indeed, when compared to a life with this sorry pair, Egypt was by far the better option. "Both of you sit down."

The men looked at each other, at the empty chairs dotted

in various locations around the room, neither being the first to move.

"Good heavens, you're acting like children." Gabriel stomped around to drag the seats in front of the desk. "Sit."

"There's no need to be so high-handed," Wellford said, directing his gaze at Gabriel while flopping down into the seat. "You're not completely innocent yourself."

Guilt flared. But the weak had a tendency to clutch at anything if it meant shifting the blame.

"I am not calculating or manipulative, and I am not too intoxicated to know better," Gabriel said. "So in comparison, whatever crime you believe me guilty of can't be all that bad."

George gave a satisfied smile. "I'm not sure Rebecca would see it that way. She seemed most upset when I told her I gave permission for you to act as her chaperone." He smiled again, wallowing in his own arrogance, knowing the news caused Gabriel's throat to constrict. "She called to see me this morning," he added.

He was lying. Gabriel had left her wearing nothing but a wrapper. He'd left her with his scent on her skin, her lips swollen and tender, her face flushed from physical exertion.

Frederick frowned. "What do you mean you gave him permission to act as a chaperone?"

"I do not need his permission to do anything," Gabriel countered. "But we are straying from the subject." He turned his attention to Frederick. "So your brother led you to believe that frightening Miss Linwood would in some way help her. It still doesn't explain why you destroyed her mother's painting."

Frederick shot to his feet. "How many times must I tell you? I did not touch the damn painting. I knew nothing about it until an hour ago. I didn't even know there was a painting."

He gave a mocking snort and jerked his head at Gabriel. "Besides, it's your fault we went there in the first place."

"It's my fault?" Gabriel said, prodding himself in the chest with his finger. "Am I to get the blame for every sorry mistake? Will no one accept responsibility for their own stupidity?"

Frederick threw himself back down in the chair. "We saw you dancing with her at the Cheltons'. I said you had a rakish look in your eye and, by living alone, Rebecca was courting trouble. I said she needed to understand the danger she was putting herself in. We wanted to check you'd not taken advantage of her, and she had gone home alone."

Gabriel paused, hearing the word that had never troubled him before, but now drove fear into his heart. "You said *we*. To whom do you refer?"

"S-surely you can't think Pennington had anything to do with it," Frederick stuttered. "The man's a decent fellow and was simply helping me out. It was just a bit of drunken foolery."

Drunken foolery!

Gabriel would never forget the look of sheer terror in Rebecca's eyes, the wet tendrils of hair stuck to her face, the way she clutched her stomach as she gasped for breath.

"Whoever damaged the painting has a personal grudge against Rebecca," he said with vehemence. "Think. Did Pennington say anything to you that sounded odd or strange?"

"No. He was surprised she was my sister, surprised she used a different name."

"He helped you break into our sister's house," Wellford said. "He must be a good friend and yet I have never heard of him. Who are his parents?"

Frederick shrugged. "How should I know? I met him at the card table a couple of months ago. Why should I give a stuff who his parents are? I'm not a chit looking to make a respectable match on the marriage mart."

Gabriel sat back in his chair and folded his arms across his chest. "Did you leave him alone while you were in her house?"

Frederick glanced up, his eyes vacant while he revisited the memory. "Yes. He was on his own for a time but—"

The riotous commotion in the hallway caught everyone's attention. No one appeared surprised when Cosgrove rapped on the door and entered. "Mrs. Stone is here to see you and has forced her way in."

What the hell did she want? If it was money why did she not just write to him as she always did?

"Mrs. Stone?" Wellford said, trying to look amused.

"My stepmother." Gabriel sighed. "It is not a good time, Cosgrove. Ask her to wait in the drawing room or better still, ask her to call again tomorrow." He had enough to deal with without listening to Sarah's woes.

"I am afraid that won't be possible, sir."

"Gabriel," Sarah panted, ducking underneath Cosgrove's arm and rushing over to the desk, leaning on the edge for support. "Quick, you must hurry."

All the gentlemen stood, and Gabriel offered the woman his chair. She was trembling, her eyes wild with panic.

"Is it Ariana?" he asked. "Has something happened?"

Sarah shook her head and glanced at the two gentlemen opposite as though seeing them for the first time. "Forgive me. I did not know you had company. Gabriel, I didn't know what else to do." A tear trickled down her cheek, and she sniffed.

"Allow me," George said, offering his handkerchief. "I am Lord Wellford, and this is my brother Frederick. We can leave the room if this is a private matter."

Sarah patted her face and then swallowed. "It's Miss Linwood," she blurted.

"Rebecca!" all three gentlemen cried simultaneously, all stepping closer to surround the hysterical woman.

"What does it have to do with Rebecca?" Gabriel asked, wondering how his stepmother even knew her name.

"At first, I thought that Ariana, well, that she was just being dramatic," Sarah said, putting her hand to her chest, "and in her excitement had simply imagined it."

"Imagined what?" Gabriel asked, his blood pumping so quickly through his veins he feared he would lash out.

"Miss Linwood took tea with us. When she left, Ariana rushed to her room to wave to her from the window. I heard her banging, heard her trying to lift the sash, shouting she'd seen a man watching the house, and he had followed Miss Linwood down the street." Sarah gasped. "The child was terrified. So I went out onto George Street hoping to spot her, hoping to reassure the child."

"Did you see her?" Wellford asked with some impatience.

"Oh, Gabriel. I saw the gentleman approach her, saw him guide her to his carriage. I called out to her, and she turned. Her face was white, ashen and then he pushed her inside, jumped in behind her and slammed the door. I ran, Gabriel. I ran as fast I could, but they were gone."

The pain was intense, sharp, stabbing him in the stomach, in the heart, robbing him of breath.

He rounded the table with lightning speed, his fist clenched and ready to end the life of anyone who got in his way. He grabbed Frederick by his coat and pulled him into his chest until their noses were touching. "You had better start bloody well talking and quick. I want to know everything about this Pennington—who he is, where he lives, what he said to you."

"It can't be him." Frederick yanked his lapel free and straightened his coat. "He didn't know who Rebecca was until I pointed her out at the Cheltons'."

Sarah Stone started sobbing, and George went to her side to offer comfort. "I suggest you tell Stone everything he wants to know, Freddie, else I'll throttle you myself."

Gabriel strode to the door and shouted his butler. When he heard the slow, methodical click of shoes on the tiled floor, he ran out into the hall. "Tell Higson to ready my carriage. Tell him to hurry."

"You can explain everything on the way," Gabriel said, returning to the room. He scoured the desk for a weapon and found an old quill knife. He wished he was as sensible as Rebecca and had a pistol in the top drawer. "We will start by visiting his lodgings, his house or wherever the hell he lives."

"What could he possibly want with Miss Linwood?" Sarah asked.

"I have no idea." Gabriel struggled to keep calm. If he were to lose Rebecca, well, the thought was so painful he could not give it merit. "But I will bleed Frederick dry until I find out."

CHAPTER 25

*H*igson raced through the streets at breakneck speed, the carriage swaying to and fro, the four occupants inside forced to hold on to the straps for fear of tumbling into a giant heap.

Gabriel turned to Freddie. "You said Chesterfield Street. Do you know what number?"

"No, but it's on the corner of Curzon. I'll know it when I see it." He glanced out of the window and then turned back. "Look, I still think you've got this all wrong. I'm certain Pennington doesn't even own a carriage. He's a decent fellow and has helped me out several times." He gave an amused snort. "Perhaps Rebecca has taken a lover, and we're chasing about London over some silly tiff. I bet they're cuddled up in his carriage, and that's why he shoved her in with such gusto."

"Rebecca has not taken a lover," Gabriel snapped, tugging on the leather strap with such force it was in danger of being ripped from its moorings.

"How do *you* know?" Freddie asked defensively.

"Rebecca always flouts the rules. She's far too independent for her own good. I wouldn't be surprised if—"

"Miss Linwood is not entertaining a lover," Sarah interjected.

Gabriel met her gaze, expecting to feel a sense of awkwardness that would force him to look away. Instead, he was surprised to find a glimmer of affection in her eyes, a look he did not deserve.

"Why would she," Sarah continued, "when she is in love with Gabriel?"

Freddie scoffed, and Gabriel's heart slammed against his ribs like a battering ram.

Weeks ago, the mere mention of love would have incited panic, would have choked the life out of him, caused him to retreat into his tomb and drag the stone lid over his sarcophagus. Yet now he wanted to bask in the warm feeling that filled his chest, let it embrace him, consume him—never let him go.

"You're mistaken," he said, doubt forcing him to hide behind a shield strong enough to ward off a Viking invasion. "We are good friends, colleagues. Rebecca displays a kindness and affection for everyone she meets."

"Not everyone," George countered. "She looked down her nose at all the gentlemen I introduced her to." He leant to his left, his cheek a mere inch from Sarah's. "I have been trying to allude to the possibility for days though he refuses to accept it."

Sarah gave an affectionate smile and whispered, "I would not normally break a confidence, not unless the situation warranted it, but Miss Linwood told me she was in love with him."

He pretended he hadn't heard them, his mind occupied with conjuring an image of Rebecca's soft lips as they formed the words, of eyes filled with desire. The pleasant dream quickly disappeared as her face turned pale and her body crumpled to the floor, devoid of life.

A coldness swept over him.

To lose Rebecca would be the end of him.

Without Rebecca, he had nothing.

The carriage was still rolling when Gabriel opened the door and, amidst the gasps and cries, jumped to the pavement. There was no time to waste, he thought, surveying the only house on the corner of Chesterfield and Curzon Street. Instinct told him it was Pennington's.

Freddie hurried to meet him, pointing to number fifteen. "This is it. I believe Pennington said the house has been converted into apartments."

"Which one's his?" Gabriel asked, scanning the numerous windows.

"How should I know? I've never been inside."

A waft of brandy drifted past Gabriel's nose. "Have you been drinking?"

Freddie shrugged. "Only a nip from a hip flask. Do you want some?"

"No, and if you don't start thinking quick, the only thing you'll be drinking is the piss from the bottom of a chamber pot."

Freddie blinked rapidly and, despite the arrival of George and Sarah, fell silent. He chewed on the corner of his bottom lip as he stared at the floor in concentration. "Wait," he said, lifting his head and pointing to the upstairs window. "It's the one on the right. I remember calling by in a hackney and he raised the sash and shouted to me."

"What now?" George asked. He turned to Sarah. "Are you sure you wouldn't prefer to wait in the carriage?"

"I couldn't possibly sit waiting while Miss Linwood is out there all alone and in need of our help. Besides, with a lady as a companion, it looks as though we're making a house call."

"She's right," Gabriel said, turning the large brass knob in the hope some fool had left it open. "It's locked."

"If we knock, someone is bound to hear us," Freddie said.

Gabriel used his weight to push against the door, but it didn't budge. "Yes, and so will everyone else on the street."

"Stand aside if you will." Higson's monotone voice caught them all off guard, and the coachman squeezed through the group. Rummaging around in the deep pocket of his overcoat, he removed a ring of keys and sifted through them. "No, not that one," he muttered trying a brass key in the door. "But this one should do it." Leaving another key in the lock, he delved into his pocket and retrieved a length of wire and after some fiddling, said, "There you go."

Without another word, and oblivious to the shocked gazes that followed him, Higson stomped back to the carriage and climbed back on top of his box.

"My word, he's a handy fellow," Freddie said. "Just the sort one needs after a night at the tables."

George sighed. "After a bottle of brandy, you mean."

"I'm fine after the first bottle," Freddie said as they entered the terrace house. "It's after the second that I struggle to get my hands in my pocket."

They made their way up the stairs and rapped lightly on the door. When Pennington failed to answer, Gabriel sent Freddie back out to fetch Higson, who came and performed the same trick with a little more ease before returning to his post.

Pennington's lodgings comprised of a large room overlooking the street, a master bedchamber with a canopy bed, a small one for guests, and a study. No doubt the owner of the property occupied the lower level apartment and provided meals upon request. A faint smell of tobacco lingered in the air, mixed with the sickly sweet smell of an excessive consumption of wine.

Gabriel made a quick scan of the rooms, to be certain there was no one home. "Take a room each," he said. "Look for anything that might relate to Rebecca, anything you think is strange, anything you feel is out of place." Noticing the crystal decanters on the sideboard, he added, "Freddie, you take the small bedchamber. George, the larger one. Sarah, will you be all right in here?"

"Don't worry about me," she said, rushing to the side table and opening the only drawer.

Gabriel strode into the study, rifled through the papers on the desk, pulled books off the shelves and shook them, flicked through the pages of a ledger.

"There's a bill here for the hire of a carriage," he shouted. "For one week dated yesterday."

Freddie raced in. "Let me see it." His eyes flitted across the crisp note, his finger following the words. "It doesn't make any sense. You think this is proof he abducted Rebecca?"

"Most definitely," Gabriel barked, feeling a rush of anger for Freddie's naivety. "But there doesn't seem to be anything else here. Nothing to explain his actions."

George and Sarah met them in the hallway.

"There's nothing of interest in his bedchamber," George said, looking forlorn. "I've even rummaged through the man's smalls."

Sarah's eyes filled with panic. "I found nothing of interest, either. Oh, Gabriel. What are we to do?"

Gabriel thrust his hand through his hair, the crippling feeling of despair causing a rush of emotion he could not suppress. "There must be something here to implicate him, something to explain his motive, some blasted clue as to where he's taken her. He's planned this and has probably been watching her for the last two days. There must be something else here other than a bloody bill."

Sarah placed her hand over her stomach as if soothing some imaginary pain. "In the carriage, you mentioned the damaged portrait. It stands to reason that Pennington is responsible. With an act so personal, you would imagine the culprit has a tangible object to focus on, to remind him of his motive, to keep the fire of vengeance burning within."

Gabriel threw his hands in the air. "Then where is it?"

"This is personal," she muttered to herself, staring at the floor. "Where does one keep their most personal items?" Her head shot up, her eyes suddenly brightening. "Show me the master chamber."

George sighed. "Aside from lifting up the floor, I've already conducted a thorough search."

Sarah patted him on the arm, and George sucked in a breath. "I know," she said, "but it would not hurt to check it again."

George bowed his head and conceded. They all congregated in the doorway of Pennington's chamber, scanning the large four-poster, the toilet stand, and the wardrobe, searching for obvious clues.

"This is ridiculous," Gabriel said, his hands clenched by his side. "God only knows what Rebecca's going through while we're standing here staring at saggy old bed drapes."

Sarah's gaze shot to the dark-green hangings. "They're not old, Gabriel. They look new."

"I'm not interested in the quality of his furnishings. All I want is to—"

"Wait!" Sarah cried, frowning as she scanned their heads.

"Gabriel, you're the tallest. Stand on that chair and see why the roof of the canopy sags in the middle."

With a disgruntled huff, Gabriel did as she asked. He reached up and stretched his arm across the top. "It's as dusty as hell up here," he said, turning his head to stifle a sneeze. "Wait, there is something here, I think I … I've got it."

Gabriel stepped down from the chair, a beaten leather satchel in his hand. He threw it on the bed. "Pennington's had this down recently as there's not a speck of dust on it." Opening the flap, he pulled out a pile of papers, a brooch, a porcelain trinket box and a book.

Sarah ran her fingers over the brooch and lingered on the red stones. "A family heirloom, perhaps?"

Gabriel shrugged and picked up the papers, flicking through a few random sketches of what appeared to be the secret musings of an artist, while the group huddled round.

"Stop," George said, peering over his shoulder. "Let me look at that one." Gabriel handed him the sketch and George studied the image. "This looks like my father, as a much younger man, but the likeness is definitely there."

"The one you're holding, my lord, is older and worn around the edges." Sarah pointed to the next sketch. "This one is much newer and drawn by a different hand, see."

Gabriel pulled it out and held it to the light. "It looks similar to the painting of Rebecca's mother. The Egyptian costume is almost identical."

"I have never seen the painting," George said, looking up. "But it looks like Rebecca to me."

"There's writing on the next one," Freddie said, glancing at the paper on top of the pile in Gabriel's hand.

Gabriel placed the sketch of Rebecca on the bed and focused his attention on Freddie's comment. "It's just a list of names. It means nothing to me. What about you?" he said, handing it to George.

George shook his head. "Out of the list of eight, two are peers, the rest I've never heard of. This fellow, Ashby, the one who has been crossed out and marked *dead*. I read recently that someone of that name died in a shooting accident at a country estate."

"I wonder what the connection is." Sarah cocked her head. "There's something written on the back."

George flipped it over, his eyes growing wide. "It's my father's name and Rebecca's mother: Dorothea Carmichael. They are both crossed out and marked as deceased. Why write *deceased* on this list and *dead* on the other?"

Sarah pointed to the names below. "Your names are listed, too, but it says Rebecca Wellford, not Linwood."

Freddie chirped up. "That's because he assumed she was a Wellford. He told me so at the Cheltons' ball. He suggested she might be ashamed to use her real name, being born out of wedlock. But I told him she just preferred anonymity."

They looked through the other sketches, all depicting various scenes of an ancient castle, the heavy use of charcoal suggesting a dark, oppressive place.

The only sheet left was a playbill for Shakespeare's *Antony and Cleopatra* staged at a playhouse in Covent Garden. Again, it was old, and Dorothea Carmichael was listed as playing the lead role.

"This is more than twenty years old," Gabriel said, handing it to Freddie. "Do you have any idea why he's kept it?"

Freddie shook his head. "No, but he went to Covent Garden after we left Rebecca's house. We'd been drinking. We tried to hail a hackney, but with the torrential rain there were none available and we ended up walking. Pennington said he'd got lucky. I assumed he meant with a woman, and he headed off for his secret rendezvous. I recall thinking it wouldn't matter if his clothes were wet as he would soon be—"

He stopped abruptly, his cheeks flushing as he glanced at Sarah.

George frowned. "There was a fire at that playhouse two days ago. It destroyed the orchestra pit. The manager put a notice in the *Times* asking for information as it started during the night. He was baffled because it didn't take out the whole building and said something about there being a series of small fires that had been put out. It's closed for a week."

The temperature in the room plummeted.

An icy chill seeped into Gabriel's bones, his body frozen by the thought of impending doom. Rebecca had been on her own with Pennington for more than an hour.

"The playhouse is closed?" Gabriel tried to suppress a shiver, tried to focus on the only thing that mattered. "Come," he said, gathering all the evidence. "There is no time to waste."

CHAPTER 26

*R*ebecca glanced out of the carriage window, surprised to find only a handful of people wandering the streets of Covent Garden. Not being fond of jeering crowds and bawdy antics, she could not recall the name of the play showing or knew why the sinister gentleman sitting opposite had stooped to such lengths to secure her company.

"Are you going to tell me what we are here to see?" she said, casting a dubious look over their inappropriate attire as the carriage stopped outside the playhouse.

He looked up at her, his eyes like small black buttons. "We are here to witness a tragedy," he said cryptically.

Rebecca doubted such a play could equal the terrifying events she'd experienced this afternoon. Yet the thought that every tragedy ended with a disastrous climax caused a strange sense of foreboding. Despite the faint whiff of dirt and urine clawing away at the back of her throat, she felt an over-whelming need to prolong her time in the carriage.

"It is one you're familiar with," he continued. "*Antony and Cleopatra.*"

He did not give her time to contemplate the coincidence. With no further explanation, he jumped from his seat and opened the door. Her heart skipped a beat as he yanked her up by the arm before pulling her down to the pavement. With the tip of the blade pressed to her back, he forced her to walk through the wrought-iron gate to a side door on the left of the building.

His free hand snaked up to the inside pocket of his brown coat. "A key in exchange for a promissory note," he said, waving it about with an air of arrogance. He rolled it into position with the tips of his fingers and then thrust it into the lock. "My skill at cards is the only good thing to come from all my years in Scotland. Your brother Frederick can testify to my claim as I have recently acquired all of his notes. I doubt he expects me to call them in."

She wondered how well he knew Frederick, wondered if conveying a level of familiarity was a part of the game.

"You mean to call in his debts?" she asked with a contemptuous snort. "You mean to ruin him?"

"I mean to show him what it's like to feel the earth fall away beneath his feet. To know how it feels when the evil hand of Fate deals a losing card."

Pain lay hidden beneath a veil of bitterness. What had roused such a depth of anger and resentment? Was it something her father had done? Was she to pay the price for someone else's crime?

"Get inside," he said, jerking his head by way of reinforcement.

Rebecca looked beyond the door to the long dingy corridor. There had been a nervous hitch in Gabriel's tone this morning, an anxious look in his eye that prompted her to carry the pistol.

If only she'd taken the time to load the damn thing.

Clutching her reticule to her chest, she took a hesitant step over the threshold, her gait unsteady and clumsy. There would be other people in the building she told herself, breathing a sigh of relief. There would be actors preparing for tonight's performance, sourcing costumes, searching for props. She would get lost amidst the bustling activity, providing the perfect opportunity to escape.

Finding the courage to continue inside, he led her down a narrow passage, to a flight of stairs that took them up to the grand lobby. The place was deathly silent. There was no sound of laughter, no echo of footsteps on the wooden stage, not even the rambling mumbles of those rehearsing their lines.

"In here," he said, pushing her through the double doors into the auditorium.

The smell of charred wood hit her immediately. Her nostrils twitched in response as her wild eyes scoured the empty room. Panic flared as she searched for some sign of movement, her chest growing tight as she shuffled past the rows of seats, the dry dust in the air making her cough.

Annoyed at her dawdling, he stepped in front and grabbed her arm, pulling her towards the burnt-out orchestra pit, to the crude flight of steps.

"If you run I will catch you," he said, dragging her up onto the stage.

Her gaze flitted about the abandoned set and then down into the pit. "We're obviously not here to see a play," she said, trying to push aside her fear.

"Oh, there will be a show, but tonight we will be the performers."

"We will perform? You said we were here to see a tragedy."

He ignored her, forced her to walk backstage to a room

halfway along the corridor. "You will find everything you need in here—costumes, powder, rouge. You have ten minutes to transform yourself into a likeness of Cleopatra."

"Cleopatra?" He wanted her to dress like an Egyptian queen. The man was a raving lunatic. "Surely you've not abducted me off the street to satisfy your love of a Shakespeare play," she said, her body growing hot, her pulse quick, as anger stamped out every other feeling and burst to the surface. "Just because my mother was an actress, it doesn't mean I know anything about acting. I don't know what strange, fanciful notion has possessed your logical mind, but you cannot just expect—"

"Shut up!" he barked, the thick green vein in his neck bulging as he flashed the knife by way of a threat. "You will do exactly as I say. Now you only have nine minutes."

With a push in the back, he forced her into the room and closed the door, leaving her alone.

Her first thought was to look for a means of escape. But after a frantic search behind rails of costumes, the curtained recess and overflowing hat stands, her efforts were in vain.

To banish the feeling of hopelessness, she took a moment to breathe, to clear her head, to think of how best to proceed. An image of Gabriel flooded her mind, of him scouting under the sheets in search of the mysterious spider, his playful smile and wandering hands leaving her feeling happy and content.

"Seven minutes."

Damn him.

"Cleopatra," she muttered to herself, moving to browse through the rail of mismatched garments. Nothing resembled the dazzling dress her mother once wore. She spotted a white Grecian style dress with a braided belt and quickly undressed and put it on. Grabbing a yellow shawl, she draped it across one shoulder, tucking it down inside the belt.

"Three minutes."

Panic set in, and she rushed to the door. "I need five more minutes," she called out to him. "There's nothing suitable, so I've had to improvise."

"You have three minutes, nothing more."

She scurried about looking for a headdress or a crown and finding nothing suitable settled on threading a beaded necklace through her hair. After powdering her face and applying rouge, she pulled the belt through the drawstring on her reticule and disguised it with the shawl.

There was no danger of the pistol blowing a hole in her foot, or in anything else for that matter, yet it might prove to be a useful deterrent.

"Time's up," he shouted, flinging the door open as she scurried back, ready to face him.

"It's the best I could come up with," she said, throwing her hands in the air.

His beady eyes scanned her from head to toe, the look of disappointment evident. "It is not as I imagined," he grumbled. "It is too virginal. It is nothing like the vibrant image hanging on your wall."

How did he know what hung on her wall?

Rebecca's hand flew to her chest, and she gasped. "It was you. You were the one who ruined my mother's painting. You broke into my home with Frederick and scared me half to death."

"It was a shame you missed the fun." He snorted. "Freddie thought you were making a fool of yourself with your Egyptian scholar and so came to snoop. I was merely hoping to cause you some distress. Discovering the painting of Dorothea Carmichael was a pleasant surprise."

Tears threatened to fall, yet she held them at bay. How could he be so callous, so cruel?

"You might have ruined my mother's portrait, but you will never ruin her memory." Then another thought struck her. "Does Frederick know what you did to the painting?"

He laughed though his face remained impassive. "The boy's a fool and often struggles to place one foot in front of the other. He has no idea I plan to destroy him, although that was before a far more rewarding prospect presented itself."

"You mean me?"

With a wave of his knife, he gestured towards the corridor. "If I were to reveal all to you now it would spoil the performance. The climax of a tragedy is far more dramatic when merged with suspense."

Moving behind her, he ushered her back to the auditorium and forced her to stand opposite him at the front of the stage.

"We will begin with the entrance of Antony and Cleopatra, or as I prefer to call it, the entrance of Lord Wellford and Miss Carmichael," he said, sounding like the narrator. "In the play, Philo explains that Antony is 'transformed into a strumpet's fool' and so that will be the basis for my story."

Rebecca stared at him, baffled as to why he intended to compare the relationship of her parents to those of characters in a Shakespeare play.

"You will play your mother," he said, his lip curling upwards to show his disdain. "You will play a harlot, a deceiver, a consummate actress whose emotion lacks any genuine warmth."

The insult caused her chest to tighten even though his description bore no resemblance to the mother she knew.

"Allow me to set the scene," he continued. "Your father is a man of prominence; a man sought after to offer guidance by the manager of a playhouse who wishes to give an authentic portrayal of Egypt."

Rebecca frowned. "You obviously know that is how my

parents met. My father helped explain the history and culture to the performers."

"Did you know your mother was not a member of the original cast? Did you know she was a late addition to the bill —an interloper?"

Rebecca shook her head. "No. I doubt they deemed it important enough to mention." The words dripped with contempt in retaliation for his insult.

"Oh, it's important," he countered, pointing the tip of the blade at her face. "My mother was cast as Cleopatra. My mother was forced to suffer the humiliation of being downgraded to the role of Octavia, forced to play a powerless woman, a woman lacking any strong emotion."

"What does that have to do with me?" she said, pushing aside the need to challenge his interpretation.

"Everything," he spat. "Your mother sauntered in like a queen of Egypt and took away everything my mother held dear. Your father was generous with his time, and my mother loved him for it. When he failed to return her affections, she admired him all the more, as a man loyal to his family. Then he took Dorothea Carmichael as his mistress, and my mother took solace in a bottle of laudanum. So you see, your father became the 'strumpet's fool' and like Mark Antony, chose desire over duty, emotion over reason."

"He could not help who he fell in love with."

"He should have bloody well helped it," he yelled, his face turning scarlet, the words exploding from his mouth with such vehemence that saliva bubbled at the corners. "That one decision ruined my life. My mother soon became addicted to laudanum, soon lost her position and took up with a Scottish laird who was more than happy to finance her addiction. She died of an overdose a few months later."

Rebecca knew the pain of losing a parent. "I'm sorry for

your loss," she said, feeling the tiniest sliver of sympathy, "but you cannot hold me responsible for that. Doing all of this will not ease the pain of your mother's death."

His face grew dark, his lids almost obscuring his black eyes. "This is not about my mother," he said, his voice slicing through the air like the swipe of his blade. "Her death pales in significance to what happened to me after that."

Rebecca examined his fine wool coat, the starched cravat tied in the latest style. This was not the figure of someone abandoned to the streets, left to pull a dust cart and scavenge for scraps.

"The laird had no real interest in my mother," he continued, "and was quick to accept me as his ward. I became the entertainment at his debauched parties. While you were educated in a host of feminine accomplishments, I became accomplished in other areas, more base, more …"

He did not complete the sentence.

"And you blame my parents for what happened?"

"I have a long list of those responsible, and I'll see vengeance brought down on every last one of them, including you. And so we come back to our play, to the final act where your suicide will avenge my mother's death."

"My suicide?" Rebecca gasped. The man was insane.

"Don't worry," he said, removing a small brown bottle from his pocket. "I'm not going to pull a poisonous asp from a fig basket. In this case, an overdose of laudanum will be far more fitting."

He would have to pin her to the floor and pour it down her throat. "Don't fool yourself into thinking it will be an act of suicide. It will be murder."

A dull thud resonated from beyond the auditorium and his gaze flew to the door. During his lapse of concentration,

Rebecca slid her fingers into her reticule and wrapped them around the handle of her pistol.

Hearing no other sound, he shook his head and turned to face her. "You will drink this," he said with a sense of urgency. "Every last drop of it."

"And if I refuse?"

He flashed the silver blade. "Then I'll gut you like a fish."

One jab was all it would take to pierce her clothing, for the blade to sink into her skin. The only hope she had was to distract him long enough to escape.

Taking a deep breath, she whipped out the pistol and with as steady a hand as she could muster, pointed it straight at his head. "Take one step closer, and I'll pull the trigger," she said, cocking it for effect.

The threat took him by surprise, and he took an awkward step back.

Then Rebecca saw a vision: an angel from Heaven in the guise of a Greek god, as Gabriel appeared in the wings, his burly coachman at his side.

CHAPTER 27

*R*ebecca was alive.

An intense feeling of euphoria flooded Gabriel's body. A giant wave of emotion scooped him up in its dizzying heights, so he felt light and free. He could have drifted along on the wave forever, but elation turned to anger as the reality of the situation brought him crashing back down to the rocky shore.

"Rebecca." Her name tumbled from his lips, the muttered whisper the only way of expressing his frustration, the only way of offering reassurance.

As though hearing the familiar sound, Rebecca glanced at the dark corridor, a look of relief flashing across her face when she spotted him. Without speaking a word, she replied. Her silent plea a distress call, piercing his heart like the razor-sharp tip of an arrow.

The muscles in his arms and legs twitched, urging him to sprint across the stage and smash his fist into Pennington's smug little face. But he saw fear in her eyes, saw that Pennington brandished a knife, and she held a pistol.

Pennington noticed her lapse in concentration and with an

accurate swipe, knocked the gun from her hand. It landed on the floor with a heavy thud. Gabriel winced as Pennington kicked it across the wooden boards, sending it skittering into the pit.

Higson placed his hand on Gabriel's arm, the claw-like grip a way of reminding him not to do anything rash, anything stupid.

The action caused him to glance at the doors of the auditorium, to where George, Frederick and Sarah were waiting for his signal. All three of them were likely to storm in at any moment without a care or thought. Indeed, Gabriel could only look on in horror as his premonition unfolded before his eyes.

Humming an old country tune that roused an image of dancing around the maypole, Sarah sauntered through the doors, her self-assured gait in harmony with her cheerful countenance.

Pennington's head turned sharply, and he focused his gaze on the merry figure skipping towards them. Without lowering his weapon, he wrapped his hand around Rebecca's wrist and tugged, drawing her closer to his body.

Gabriel gritted his teeth. The need to rip the man's head from his shoulders was overwhelming.

"We're closed," Pennington growled in a menacing tone.

"I know." Sarah pulled off her gloves. "We're rehearsing today for *The Virgin Unmasked,* but I don't remember there being a scene with a knife."

"There's been a fire," Pennington said sternly. "There's no need to come in today. Go home."

"No one told me. I was told I need to work on my delivery. Apparently, my laugh is unnatural." She jerked her head towards the door as she walked down the aisle. "The others will be along in a minute."

Like a rabbit trapped in a snare, Pennington's head moved

back and forth, his limbs jerking in response. After a moment, he appeared to regain his confidence and said, "Then you had better come and join us on stage."

Sarah's mask fell, uncertainty causing her to hesitate. "I'll just sit here and wait for the others," she said, sliding into one of the rows. "I'm losing my voice, and if I overdo it, there'll be hell to pay."

Pennington narrowed his gaze, the corner of his mouth curving up. "I'm not a fool. I'm familiar enough with actresses to know you're not one. You're the woman on George Street. What I don't know is how you knew we were here."

Sarah studied him, and Gabriel could almost hear the cogs turning. "We know all about you," she said. "We know all about your obsession." She turned her head and called out over her shoulder. "You can come in now."

The doors burst open. George and Frederick Wellford stormed into the room, their hands clenched by their sides, their faces red and puffy.

"Ah, Freddie, it's a little early in the day for you," Pennington cried. "At this time, I'd expect you to be crawling out of your bed in a drunken stupor, wiping vomit off your chin."

"You bloody liar," Freddie yelled. "If there were no ladies present, I'd say something a damn sight harsher. I thought we were friends."

"I'm no one's friend. A fact you would have discovered when I called in your promissory notes."

Freddie's face blanched. "But you said—"

"I lied. I do not have time to explain the dastardly plans I had for you," Pennington said, yanking Rebecca's arm. "Now, thanks to your father's by-blow here, I get to exact the perfect revenge. I must thank you, Freddie. Had you not pointed out the fact that Miss Linwood was your sister, I would never have made the connection."

George spoke up as he shuffled closer. "Revenge for what?"

"For everything," he sneered, pulling Rebecca to his chest and pressing the knife against her throat. "Do not come any closer, not unless you want to see her blood splattered across the stage."

Gabriel flinched, his head throbbing with uncontrollable rage while his body felt weak and helpless.

"Wait," Higson whispered, holding Gabriel back. "This'll be his only way out. Best we keep out of view."

"You won't get away with this," George cried. "I swear to you, I will hunt you down. I will make your life a living hell."

Pennington bared his teeth. "There are worse places. I should know. Nothing you could do to me could be any worse than the nightmare I've already lived."

Holding Rebecca tight against his chest, Pennington shuffled back across the stage. "If you follow us, I'll kill her."

They were almost out of view when Sarah cried, "We've seen the names on your list, and we've seen your sketches. We know what you plan to do and will inform all those mentioned. They will come for you. They will track you down."

Pennington froze, his face turning deathly pale. "Y-you can't," he mumbled. "You have no right."

"I have the list right here," George said, tapping his chest. "I will offer you a trade."

Pennington lowered the knife and shoved Rebecca forward. "Give it to me," he demanded, yet fear seemed to form the basis of his emotion. "Bring it here to the front or I will kill her."

George made no argument and sauntered down to the

stage. Reaching into his pocket, he removed a folded note. "Here," he said, "now let her go."

Relaxing his hold on Rebecca, Pennington bent forward and snatched the note. At the same time, Gabriel charged him from behind, delivering a powerful blow to his right kidney.

The knife fell to the floor as Pennington's knees buckled underneath him and he sagged down into a heap, howling in pain.

Rebecca scrambled away to the opposite end of the stage as Gabriel picked Pennington up by the collar of his coat, swung him round and punched him on the nose. He heard the sound of the bone cracking before he saw the blood and as Gabriel pulled his arm back to deliver another jab, Higson rushed to his shoulder.

"We'll deal with this scoundrel, sir," he said, grabbing Pennington by the upper arm as though he were a flimsy doll. "You see to Miss Linwood."

Gabriel blinked rapidly, his anger subsiding as he turned to face Rebecca. The strange emotion that bubbled away in his stomach erupted in a rush of longing, desire … of love.

She returned his gaze, her eyes brimming with tears, and as he strode towards her, she ran and jumped into his arms. "Oh, Gabriel. I thought I'd never see you again."

Forgetting they were not alone, he rained kisses over her face, caressed her back and smoothed out her hair. The feel of her soft, pliant body soothed his soul. "If I'd lost you," he said, shaking his head as he could not bear to contemplate the possibility.

Unable to cope with the flood of emotion, he did the only thing he knew would bring comfort: he pulled her tighter to his chest, his mouth settling on hers with overwhelming urgency. The need to taste her, to get lost in her mouth, drowned out every other thought.

She did not protest, even when Pennington released a tirade of abuse as he was dragged from the room.

George cleared his throat, forcing Gabriel to tear his lips away and look down. "We'll need your carriage," he said with a disapproving glare. "Freddie said the hired coach has disappeared, and we cannot risk Pennington escaping."

"Very well. I will see Rebecca and Sarah safely home. I'll call on you in the morning." Gabriel added no further explanation. Naturally, he would want to know what happened to Pennington, and he would need to make a formal statement. In light of the fact that he held Rebecca in a passionate clinch, he knew George would expect some form of declaration. "Don't forget the list," Gabriel added, gesturing to the crumpled note lying on the floor.

"That's not the list. That's my tailor's bill," George replied with a smirk as he picked it up and moved to walk away.

"George." Rebecca called out to him, the word revealing a hint of tenderness. "I know what Pennington's done, but I don't want him to hang."

His mouth fell open as he arched a brow. "The decision is not mine to make. He'll be committed for trial. It will depend upon the evidence," he said, offering a weak smile.

Based on the evidence, Gabriel knew the man would most certainly hang.

George's gaze drifted to Sarah, and he strode over to her, took her bare hand and brought it to his lips. "It was a pleasure to meet you, Mrs. Stone," he said, lingering for longer than necessary before turning on his heels and marching from the room.

Sarah's cheeks flushed a bright shade of crimson, and as she climbed the steps to the stage, she struggled to make eye contact. "Come," she said, glancing up at Rebecca. "I will help you change out of your costume."

Rebecca took Sarah's hands and held them. "I cannot thank you enough. If you had not run after the carriage. If you had not gone to Gabriel, then …"

Sarah pulled her into an embrace.

To give them some privacy, Gabriel dropped down into the pit to search for the pistol. He heard them whispering and Rebecca's sly glance told him they were speaking about him.

"Your pistol, m'lady," Gabriel said, returning to Rebecca's side. "Thank goodness you didn't get a chance to fire the thing."

"Oh, it's not loaded," she said. "I was in too much of a hurry this morning."

He arched a brow. "Yes, I hear you've been very busy."

Rebecca's mouth fell open, and Gabriel tapped her chin to close it.

Gabriel turned to his stepmother. "Rebecca is right, Sarah. I cannot thank you enough for everything you've done. I was ready to leave Pennington's apartment, yet you encouraged me to keep searching." He nodded towards the door of the auditorium. "It was a courageous thing to do, to walk in here on your own, and I can't wait to see you perform in *The Virgin Unmasked*."

Sarah laughed. "I would do anything for my family, Gabriel, but I draw the line at being pelted with rotten apples."

Rebecca threaded her arm through Gabriel's and squeezed. "When we take you home, Sarah, would you mind if we called in to see Ariana? We will not stay long. I believe she will be surprised to find that her brother has finally returned from his tour of Egypt."

Gabriel glanced at Rebecca, who offered him an innocent

smile, and then at Sarah, who was busy trying to disguise her trembling lip. For some reason, the thought of spending time with them didn't bother him as it used to. Surprisingly, he'd grown fond of Sarah in the few hours they'd spent together, and he would always be indebted to her for helping him find Rebecca.

"We would only stay long enough to take tea," he said, "or perhaps something a little stronger. And on the way, you can tell me why I'm supposed to be in Egypt."

CHAPTER 28

They stayed with Sarah and Ariana for two hours. The child soon forgot her distress and was happy to have her mother home, even more delighted to see her brother at long last.

Rebecca choked back the tears when Ariana ran into Gabriel's arms, and she found she loved him all the more for not showing the slightest sign of awkwardness.

When he regaled tales of a boisterous camel and of a pilfering monkey who'd stolen a fig from his plate, she laughed with them, even though she knew it was all a figment of his wild imagination.

"Ariana is a wonderful child," Rebecca said. "I find her laugh infectious." She gripped Gabriel's arm as he escorted her to the front door of the museum. As the hour was late, it had long since been vacated by the day's visitors.

He chuckled in response, his eyes warm and inviting and she wanted to press her body against his, thrust her hands into his hair, claim his mouth and devour him.

"I had forgotten how affectionate she can be."

Rebecca smiled, her heart singing the sweetest song.

Would there ever be a time when she did not feel a desperate ache in her chest whenever she looked at him?

"I thought we would have to drag her arms from around your neck. Indeed, I believe she loves you almost as much as I do."

Gabriel froze, stared into her eyes and then down at the floor. "Rebecca, I …"

She knew the declaration would surprise him, but she was tired of hiding her true feelings. "Oh, don't be coy. Sarah told me what she said to you although you would need to be blind not to notice." She slid her hand into his. The heat radiating from his palm sent tingles shooting up her arm as she pulled him towards the door. "Will you stay with me tonight?"

"I'm surprised you need to ask."

Desire unfurled in response to his rich, sensual tone. "Well, it would not do to be too presumptuous."

They made their way inside, his gaze searching, assessing, never leaving her.

"After such a terrifying ordeal you must be famished," he said, bringing her fingers to his lips and brushing a gentle kiss on top. "Shall I go to the kitchen? Mrs. James must still be here."

Feeling tired and exhausted, Rebecca shook her head. "I've no appetite. But you go. Help yourself to whatever you can find."

As if on cue, a growl rumbled from his stomach.

"Your body is in desperate need of sustenance," she continued with a chuckle, aware that he was the only sustenance she needed. "I must wash and change and then I'll join you at the table."

She moved to walk upstairs, but he caught her by the hand and pulled her into an embrace. "Tell me you've changed your mind about Egypt," he said, his hot breath caressing her cheek as he brushed a loose tendril back behind her ear. "Tell me you'll stay here at the museum where you belong."

If only he had said "stay with me" then she would never have refused him.

Rebecca wound her arms around his neck and kissed him until their tongues were lost in each other's mouths. She kissed him until their breathing grew ragged and their bodies burned with passion.

"I can't tell you that, Gabriel," she said, lowering her hands so they lay flat against his chest. The steady beat of his heart pulsed beneath her palm. "But know I am deeply in love with you. Know there will never be another, only you."

He swallowed visibly, his eyes brimming with emotion. But she stepped away, and he watched her walk up the stairs.

Once in her room, she stripped off her clothes down to her chemise, soaked a linen square in a bowl of cold water and wiped over her neck and face with long massaging strokes.

It was hard to believe that only this morning she'd sat at her mirror unaware of Pennington's devious plans for revenge. His acrid smell still clung to her skin. The urge to scrub, to remove every trace, was impossible to ignore. Topping up the bowl, she rubbed away at her skin again until it prickled from the abrasive movements. The uncomfortable feeling forced her to acknowledge the reality of the situation.

If Gabriel hadn't saved her, she would most probably be dead.

Tears filled her eyes, her hands trembling at the thought, her airway closing as she sucked in a breath. She tried to concentrate on something tangible; on all the things she should be grateful for—Gabriel, her antiquities, even her brothers. The memory of all those who'd come to her rescue banished all negative thoughts. The feeling that she should use the experience to her advantage, to forge ahead with her plans for the future, suddenly pushed to the fore.

Only one question remained: Should she plan for a future that included Gabriel?

Part of her wanted to tell him she would stay at home and not travel to Egypt. She would be here whenever he needed her. The lure of the exotic was nothing compared to the lure of being with him. But what if he struggled to commit? What if this was just a fleeting dalliance?

Feeling a deep ache in her chest, she slapped her hand over her heart, lay down on the bed and closed her eyes. The pain of contemplating a life without him was beyond anything she'd ever felt before.

Her mind wandered, imagined a life where they lived together, an erotic fantasy of amorous frolicking, of gratifying indulgence, of love, of a home and family. They were together always, forever. As her breathing slowed, she sank deeper into the blissful world, got lost in the beautiful dream.

With a heavy heart, Gabriel climbed the stairs, but there was no sign of Rebecca. Plate in hand, he walked down to her bedchamber and knocked gently. When she failed to answer, he eased the door away from the jamb and peered inside the dimly lit room.

Rebecca lay on the bed, dressed in nothing but her chemise. The soft rise and fall of her chest suggested she'd fallen asleep.

He entered the room and closed the door, put his cold platter on the small table and walked around the bed to stand at her side.

She looked ethereal, magical, her vibrant copper tresses spilling onto the coverlet in soft waves. Even in sleep, she appeared happy and content, the soothing sound of her breathing calling out to him like a siren's song.

Good God, he'd never loved anything more in his entire life.

He was a bloody fool!

He should have told her how he felt when he had the chance, but a surge of raw emotion had hit the back of his throat, and all coherent words were lost to him.

Moving to the opposite side of the bed, he pulled down the coverlet and then returned to Rebecca, scooping her up in his arms with the intention of putting her into bed.

As he lowered her down, she gave a pleasurable hum. "I love you," she whispered before turning on her side and cuddling into the pillow.

With a lump in his throat, he pulled the covers up around her shoulders and stroked her hair. "And I love you," he whispered in reply.

It felt good to say the words aloud, to acknowledge the depth of his feelings. Indeed, it took a tremendous amount of effort not to wake her and declare it a hundred times over.

He'd often wondered if such an intense physical desire would naturally progress into love. He'd wondered if the ache in his loins would become an ache in his heart, as though the two things were separate. Now, he knew the two were woven together. His body throbbed at the thought of joining with her. His heart rejoiced at the prospect.

After finishing his meal, he stripped off his clothes and climbed into bed, his manhood stirring in response to the intimacy of the action. When her hand fluttered over his chest, she snuggled into him, and he clenched his teeth as he fought back the demands of his body.

Suffice to say, he struggled to sleep, his mind preoccupied with thoughts of the future, thoughts that did little to dampen his desire. When dawn came, he climbed out of bed, dressed quickly and went in search of paper and an inkwell.

Scrawling a note for Rebecca to meet him in Hanover Square at noon, Gabriel waited for Mrs. James to return, giving her the letter and specific instructions before leaving.

It was ten o'clock by the time he left George Wellford's house. On his return to Hanover Square, Cosgrove gave no indication that his master's absence was anything out of the ordinary.

"When Miss Linwood arrives you're to escort her down into the cellar."

For a second, Cosgrove's eyes widened, and then he blinked, the hooded lids falling back into place. "To the cellar, sir," he reiterated, his tone absent of any inflection.

"I don't have much time," Gabriel said, shrugging out of his coat. "But I'll need some boxes or old crates, anything you can lay your hands on. Bring them down to me." Gabriel raced past Cosgrove and shouted over his shoulder, "And tell Higson I'll need his help."

He set about clearing out the cellar, packaged up all his notes and put them in a box. "Put this one in my study," he said as Higson came plodding back into the room. "Leave the equipment in the crate and I'll donate it to one of the scientific societies at the University."

Higson nodded. "Miss Linwood has arrived. She's waiting upstairs."

Gabriel brushed the dust from his waistcoat and ran his fingers through his hair. "Ask her to come down, would you, Higson?"

Taking a deep breath to calm the pounding in his chest, he stood next to the long table. Deciding his stance was similar to a dignitary posing for a portrait, he moved to the door, just as she appeared at the bottom of the stairs.

He felt awkward, nervous, but then she smiled.

"So this is the mysterious cellar that has kept you a prisoner for so long." She walked into the room and glanced at the empty shelves. "I'm a little disappointed. I was expecting to find you wrist-deep in a gruesome experiment."

"Last week, perhaps. This week I am a changed man."

"I rather liked the old one."

"You'll like the new one much more."

"Are you going somewhere?" She looked down at the crate full of scientific equipment.

"That all depends on you."

His hands throbbed with the need to touch her. He walked over to her and untied the ribbons on her bonnet. With keen interest, she watched his fingers move deftly. After placing the item on the table, he worked on removing her gloves.

"My heart is all a flutter, Mr. Stone," she said, the seductive lilt unmistakable. "As I wonder what devilish experiment you have in store for me."

"Oh, I have plenty of things in store for you, Miss Linwood." He kissed her then, hard and quick, as he wouldn't be able to stop himself if he did anything more lascivious. "Marry me," he whispered. "Say you'll be my wife, Rebecca."

Her hand flew up to cover her mouth; her eyes grew wide with surprise. "Marry you? Gabriel, if this is because you don't want me to go to Egypt then there's no need to—"

"This is not about your trip to Egypt." He grabbed her by her elbows and drew her closer. "Rebecca, I'm in love with you. I've been in love with you since you sauntered into Banbury's library and attempted to describe the uses of a lectern. Even before that. Since you sat in protest on my front steps and waved at every passer-by."

She dropped her hand as her eyes welled with tears. "Do you mean it, Gabriel? Tell me I'm not asleep in my bed dreaming."

"I will spend the rest of my life showing you how much I mean it. We will go to Egypt together. We'll ride camels across the desert, eat exotic fruit so I'm forced to lick the juice from your lips, roll about naked in a tent."

She gave a little chuckle. "Well, you certainly appear to have thought it through."

He'd spent the night with a throbbing erection and thought of nothing else. "And when you want to come home, I'll live with you, or you can live here, or we'll buy a new house together."

She placed her hand on his cheek. "I love you."

"Rebecca, I love you so much it's killing me. I'm done with all of this," he said, waving his hand at the room. "I want to start again, with you."

She turned away from him, walked over to the door and a pain with the force of a lightning bolt shot through his heart. Pulling the key from the front of the door, she closed it, thrust it into the hole in the back and locked them in.

"You know, my bedchamber used to be a place of night-mares," she said, undoing the buttons on her jacket and shrugging out of it. "Whenever I thought of going in there, I'd feel cold shivers running down my spine. That was until we spent the night in my bed and the morning looking for spiders. Now I feel shivers for an entirely different reason."

She removed the pins from her hair and let it tumble around her shoulders. He tried to follow her train of thought, but desire burst forth in all its wondrous glory.

"What are you saying?"

"I'm saying I want to start again, with you. I want to marry you, Gabriel." She moved to undo the buttons on his waistcoat. "I want to travel to Egypt with you. I want to help you banish the ghosts of the past, starting with this room."

When she yanked his shirt over his head and ran her fingers through the hair on his chest, he took her mouth in a desperate frenzy. "Have I told you I love you?" he muttered, dragging his mouth away to rain kisses down her neck.

"Yes," she panted, the tips of her fingers grazing his nipples. "But I would like to hear it fall from your lips during the throes of passion."

"Do that again and I will shout loud enough to wake the pharaohs from their tombs."

The End